SPY PUPS

SURVIVAL CAMP

ANDREW COPE

Illustrated by James de la Rue

PUFFIN

PUFFIN BOOKS

Published by the Penguin Group
Penguin Books Ltd, 80 Strand, London WC2R ORL, England
Penguin Group (USA) Inc., 375 Hudson Street, New York, New York 10014, USA
Penguin Group (Canada), 90 Eglinton Avenue East, Suite 700, Toronto, Ontario, Canada M4P 2Y3
(a division of Pearson Penguin Canada Inc.)
Penguin Ireland, 25 St Stephen's Green, Dublin 2, Ireland
(a division of Penguin Books Ltd)
Penguin Group (Australia), 250 Camberwell Road, Camberwell, Victoria 3124, Australia
(a division of Pearson Australia Group Pty Ltd)
Penguin Books India Pvt Ltd, 11 Community Centre, Panchsheel Park, New Delhi – 110 017, India
Penguin Group (NZ), 67 Apollo Drive, Rosedale, Auckland 0632, New Zealand
(a division of Pearson New Zealand Ltd)
Penguin Books (South Africa) (Pty) Ltd, 24 Sturdee Avenue, Rosebank, Johannesburg 2196, South Africa

Penguin Books Ltd, Registered Offices: 80 Strand, London WC2R ORL, England

puffinbooks.com

First published 2012
This edition produced for The Book People Ltd,
Hall Wood Avenue, Haydock, St Helens, WA11 9UL
1

Text copyright © Andrew Cope and Ann Coburn, 2012
Illustrations copyright © James de la Rue, 2012
All rights reserved

The moral right of the authors and illustrator has been asserted

Set in Bembo
Typeset by Palimpsest Book Production Limited, Falkirk, Stirlingshire
Made and printed in Great Britain by Clays Ltd, St Ives plc

British Library Cataloguing in Publication Data
A CIP catalogue record for this book is available from the British Library

ISBN: 978-0-141-34550-5

www.greenpenguin.co.uk

MIX
Paper from
responsible sources
FSC
www.fsc.org   FSC™ C018179

Penguin Books is committed to a sustainable
future for our business, our readers and our planet.
This book is made from Forest Stewardship
Council™ certified paper.

ALWAYS LEARNING   **PEARSON**

Contents

1. The Beast

Gaz Guzzler waddled into the biggest room in his mansion and got ready to sit down. For him, this was not an easy task. The seat of his favourite armchair was extra wide, but his massive bottom was even wider. He backed into position and then squatted with his hands on his knees like a sumo wrestler.

'Ghaahh!' he grunted, pushing his enormous left bum cheek down first. The chair shuddered. Gaz took a breath and got to work on his equally enormous right bum cheek. 'Neeyaaghh!'

The chair groaned. Gaz turned red in the face. Finally his backside settled on to the cushion. He was in! With a contented sigh, he opened the fridge built into the left arm of his chair, pulled out a slice of triple chocolate cheesecake and took a huge bite. In front of him, three floor-to-ceiling windows looked out on to a beautiful lake surrounded by forests and mountains, but Gaz Guzzler was not interested in the view. He pressed a button on the control panel in the armrest of his chair and a monitor screen rose up from beneath the floor. It showed a rocky chamber, filled with dust and noise and men in hard hats.

Gaz Guzzler chomped on his cheesecake as he watched the on-screen activity. He wasn't sure whether his smile was because of the cheesecake or the fact that the men were all working very hard. Two were hacking chunks from the chamber wall, and more were hauling the rubble to a workbench, where a man with 'Pete' written on his helmet was checking every rock.

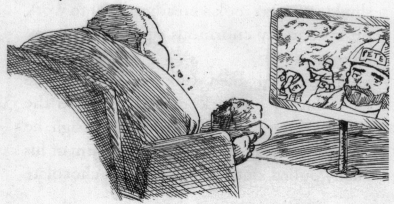

PUFFIN BOOKS

SPY PUPS
SURVIVAL CAMP

I grew up in a family that always had pets. My little sis had a rabbit called Rosie and a guinea pig called Benji. And we had a dog called Bruce. And then another called Jasper. We had a pink cat called Monty. None of them could ride a bike, send an email, play the piano or do ballroom dancing.

And then we adopted a black and white dog called Lara. To be honest, she's not the best-looking canine in the world. She's got one silly sticky-up ear and a sort of vacant expression. But I could have sworn I saw her driving my car? And I'm pretty sure she was wearing shades?

I can only assume I was imagining it.

If you want Lara or her puppy to visit your school, please email her at lara@artofbrilliance.co.uk. They'll probably have to bring Andrew Cope along too, but don't let that put you off. Or you can find out more about the Spy Dog and Spy Pups books online at *www.spydog451.co.uk*, where there are pictures, videos and competitions too!

Books by Andrew Cope

Spy Dog
Spy Dog Captured!
Spy Dog Unleashed!
Spy Dog Superbrain
Spy Dog Rocket Rider
Spy Dog Teacher's Pet

Spy Pups Treasure Quest
Spy Pups Prison Break
Spy Pups Circus Act
Spy Pups Danger Island
Spy Pups Survival Camp

Spy Dog Joke Book

Suddenly, Pete gave a yell and all work stopped in the chamber. Gaz stuffed the remaining cheesecake into his mouth and leant forward as far as his belly would allow. For a few seconds, everyone was still. Pete stared at the rock in his hand, the men stared at Pete, and Gaz stared at the screen. Then Gaz ran out of patience. He gave an impatient snort, causing slimy blobs of chewed-up cheesecake to shoot out of his nose, and pressed the intercom button on his control pad.

'Report!' he spluttered.

Pete looked up at the camera on the chamber wall. 'Just let me make sure, Mr Guzzler.' He poured water over the rock to wash away the dust. A fat vein of gold gleamed up at him. 'Yes,' he said, with a relieved smile. 'It's here, Mr Guzzler. Exactly where you said it would be.'

'Of course it is, you idiot!' said Gaz. 'I'm never wrong. Now stop wasting time and get Project Midas underway!'

'But – we can't go any further, Mr Guzzler. Not without the beast.'

Gaz gave a roar of frustration. He was not used to waiting. In the seven years since he'd won the lottery with the first ticket he'd ever bought, he had always got exactly what he wanted, exactly when he wanted.

Pete flinched but stood his ground. 'I'm sorry, Mr Guzzler, sir, but we must wait. If we go on alone without the beast to protect us, we might die.'

'Oh, you're such big babies!' huffed Gaz. 'All right, keep your nappy on. The beasty-weasty is on its way. It'll arrive tomorrow night. Until then, you lot can make yourselves useful by cleaning every single one of my fifty cars, trucks, quads and motorbikes.'

He hit the button and Pete was cut off in mid-thanks. As the monitor screen sank back into the floor, Gaz's stomach gave a volcanic rumble. Good news always made him hungry. So did bad news, sad news and funny news. He opened his fridge, pulled out a sandwich box and looked inside. His face darkened.

'Mum!' he bellowed. 'MUMMEEEE!!!'

The door flew open and a thin, worried-looking woman hurried in. 'Yes, son?'

Gaz threw the lunchbox at her, scattering salad leaves across the room. 'Salad!' he roared.

'You gave me salad!'

'It's good for you, Garry,' quavered Mrs Guzzler, picking a spring onion out of her hair.

'How many times?' growled Gaz. 'I don't do green. Get it?'

'Yes, dear.'

'Come on,' said Gaz. 'We're going out.' He pulled a lever on the side of his chair and, with a groan of springs, the seat tilted forward, pushing him up on to his feet.

'A nice walk, maybe?' said Mrs Guzzler timidly, eyeing his enormous belly. 'I saw an otter down by the lake earlier. And the forest is looking lovely.'

'I told you, I don't do green. Have my newest monster truck brought round to the front of the house. I fancy a deep-fried pizza.'

2. Brake Time!

Lara gave Professor Cortex an anxious look. Her old friend had been trained by MI6 to resist interrogation, but she could see that he was near to breaking point. Sweat was trickling down his face and his hands were shaking. For hours, he had been strapped to a seat and pinched, poked and battered, while his interrogator asked him the same question over and over again.

Strapped in tight beside him, Lara could do nothing to help. 'Hold on, Prof!' she barked. 'You've lasted longer than most!'

Professor Cortex gasped as his interrogator doused him in icy liquid and then leant in close to his ear. He gritted his teeth, waiting for the question that would surely follow.

'ARE WE NEARLY THERE YET?'

'Careful with that cold lemonade, Ollie,' said Mr Cook from the front passenger seat of the car. 'You've spilt it all over the professor! Sit properly, please.'

'Sorry,' said Ollie, elbowing Professor Cortex in the ribs as he flung himself back into his seat. 'But are we –?'

'Yes, Ollie. We're nearly there,' said Mrs Cook, checking her driver's satnav. 'Only another five miles to Clearwater Village.'

'Thank goodness,' groaned Professor Cortex, prising popcorn out of his ear. He was one of the world's top scientists and the head of the British Government's animal spying programme, but a few hours in a car with six-year-old Ollie had nearly finished him.

Lara gave him a sympathetic lick. 'I did try to warn you,' she woofed, remembering the scene outside the Cooks' house earlier that day.

Professor Cortex had arranged an all-expenses-paid long weekend in the Lake District for the whole family. It was his way of saying sorry for repeatedly putting the three Cook children, Ben, Sophie and Ollie, into danger.

Not to mention my pups, thought Lara, turning

her head to gaze fondly at Star and Spud, curled up in a nest of blankets in the back of the car.

As instructed, the Cook family, along with Lara, Spud and Star, had been packed and ready to go by the time the Secret Service van pulled up outside the house. Agents T and K, the professor's personal bodyguards, had been dressed, as always, in black suits and shades, but Professor Cortex had clambered out of the van wearing a pair of ancient, baggy hiking shorts. Star had giggled, nudging her brother.

'Whoa! Look at those mushroom-white legs!'

'Agghh! The glare!' Spud had yelped, slapping his front paws over his eyes.

'Shorts, Professor?' Ben had said, in a strangled voice.

'I thought they deserved an outing,' Professor Cortex had said, pointing at his legs. 'The poor things spend most of their time in secret underground laboratories. Not much sun down there.'

'Not much sun in the Lake District either,' Sophie had pointed out. 'My geography teacher says it's one of the rainiest places in England.'

'Not this weekend,' Professor Cortex had said cheerfully. 'On the way here, I connected to one of our satellites. According to our van monitor screens, there's not a single cloud over the Lake District.'

Ben had looked enviously at the sleek, black Secret Service van. He was twelve and fascinated with technology. 'Monitor screens with satellite connections? I wouldn't mind riding up to the Lake District in that.'

'Me too,' Sophie had chipped in. 'I always get sick in the back of the car.'

'Go ahead,' Professor Cortex had said,

waving them towards the van. 'There's plenty of room for both of you in the front, alongside my agents. I'll ride in the back of your car with Oliver and Lara. How about that, young man?'

'Yes!' Ollie had cried, bouncing along the pavement and falling into the hedge.

'No!' Lara had woofed. 'Don't do it, Prof!' She had pointed at Ollie and then given an Oscar-worthy impersonation of a karate fight, a tap dance and a tornado, all rolled into one. *Four hours! With Ollie. It'll be torture!*

I couldn't have been any clearer, Lara thought now, still slightly hurt that Professor Cortex had not understood her warning about Ollie. *Oh well. At least his act of self-sacrifice should make Mrs Cook thaw out a bit.* She glanced hopefully at the rear-view mirror, but Mrs Cook's eyes were looking as frosty as ever.

Poor Professor Cortex, thought Lara. *I understand why Mrs Cook is so angry; after all, I'm a mum too. But it's not all his fault. Last time we got into danger, the prof wasn't even there!* Her eyes grew serious as she remembered their family summer holiday on Pleasure Island. They had run into some old enemies – Jimmy Tartan and Mr Big – and Spud had nearly died as a result. *Not good!*

Lara sighed. The truth was that when the Cook family had adopted her a few years ago, they had adopted danger too. Back then, she had still been in active service as the world's first ever Spy Dog, trained by Professor Cortex. 'Lara' had stood for Licensed Assault and Rescue Animal, and her code name had been GM451. Now she was retired. *And not a moment too soon*, she thought, looking at herself in the rear-view mirror. The bullet hole clean through the middle of her sticky-up ear was a chilling reminder of the dangers of being a Spy Dog.

Unfortunately, her pups seemed determined to follow in her paw prints. Spud already had a matching bullet hole through his ear from an earlier adventure, and now he and Star had both just qualified as fully fledged Spy Dogs. Lara was beginning to realize that she could not stand in their way, but she had insisted that they be given more specialist training before they began active service. Professor Cortex had agreed, starting with some survival training this weekend. While Mr and Mrs Cook enjoyed a luxury spa hotel, and she kept an eye on the Cook children at the Tall Trees Outward Bound Centre, her pups would be camping out in the forest with a former SAS man known only as 'X'. *That should give them enough adventure to keep them happy for a while*, thought Lara.

'Nearly there, Ma!' yapped Spud, standing on his hind legs and putting his paws on the back of Lara's seat. 'Clearwater Lake should be just round this corner. I can't wait! Come on, Sis! Shake a leg!'

Star took off her headphones and jumped up from their nest of blankets to join her brother. She had spent the journey learning to speak Otterese.

'I hope we find an otter,' said Star, scrambling up next to Spud.

'I hope we find a good cake shop,' replied Spud, with a doggy grin.

'I don't think there are many cake shops in the forest,' woofed Lara.

'Never mind,' said Spud, laying a paw on his bulging rucksack. 'I'm well stocked with food supplies.'

Lara looked proudly at her pups as they hung over the back of the seat, tails wagging furiously. Star was black and white with one sticky-up ear, just like her. She was very hard-working and had done well in all her Spy School studies, especially fitness training, where she had proved that she could run as far and as fast as a fully grown dog. Already, she was losing her puppy fat and developing the slim build of an athlete. *Just like me*, thought Lara, sitting up straighter and sucking in her tummy.

Spud had shiny black fur, the same as his father, Potter. He could never be called slim or fast, but he was strong and good at martial arts. He was a natural with gadgets and his curious nature meant that he was brilliant at solving mysteries. *He loves a good puzzle*, thought Lara. *Again, just like me.*

The car turned a corner and, suddenly, there were Clearwater Village and Clearwater Lake spread out before them. Everyone gasped.

'Oh, it's beautiful!' cried Mrs Cook, slowing the car to get a better look.

'Windsurfers!' Ollie yelled at the top of his voice, making Professor Cortex wince. 'Watch me, Prof!' He yanked his sweatshirt off and pretended to windsurf with it.

'Wow!' yelped Star, watching the bright sails skim across the lake. 'I can't wait to try that!'

'And I can't wait to try that!' woofed Spud, spotting a pizza restaurant just ahead.

'There's your luxury spa hotel, Mr and Mrs Cook,' said Professor Cortex, pointing to a stylish building on the water's edge. He was hoping it might earn him some brownie points.

'Very nice!' said Mr Cook, rubbing his hands together.

'Look, Mum!' yelled Ollie. 'Look at the hotel pool!'

'I can't look just now, Ollie,' said Mrs Cook. 'I'm driving.'

'But it's massive!' Ollie flung his arms apart and his sweatshirt flew from his hand. It landed on Mrs Cook's head, covering her eyes. As she fumbled with her blindfold, a bright red monster truck drove out of a side road right in front of her and then stopped dead outside the pizza restaurant.

'Look out! We're going to crash into it!' barked Lara.

'Leave this to me, Ma!' yelped Spud, shooting between the front seats like a puppy cannonball. With a second to spare, he landed bottom-first on the brake pedal.

Thud!

The car screeched to a very sudden stop.

'Spud! What on earth . . .?' began Mrs Cook,

pulling the sweatshirt off her head and blinking down at him. Then she looked through the windscreen. 'Oh, my . . .'

A metal tow bar glinted in the sun centimetres from her nose. Behind the tow bar, a number plate loomed.

GUZZLER50

The monster-truck cab sat so high on its huge wheels that the bonnet of their car had slid underneath the back bumper. Spud had hit the brake just in time before the truck's tow bar smashed through their windscreen.

'Well done, Spud!' yapped Star, poking her

head over the back seat. 'You really slammed that brake pedal!'

'It's my secret weapon,' woofed Spud, waggling his plump bottom. 'The rear to fear!'

3. Litter Lout

Mrs Cook backed out from underneath the monster truck and reversed down the road to the spa hotel. The Secret Service van pulled up behind them and everyone jumped out.

'That was close!' cried Ben. 'Are you OK?'

'We're fine,' said Mr Cook. 'Spud saved the day.'

'Well done, Spud,' said Sophie, crouching down and giving him a hug.

'I only sat down hard,' wagged Spud modestly.

'Sorry, Mum,' said Ollie, looking at his feet.

Mrs Cook ruffled his hair. 'Not your fault' she soothed.

Just then, the monster truck's front passenger door opened and a thin, anxious-looking woman climbed down the steps from the cab and hurried into the pizza restaurant.

'Look at those massive wheels!' said Ollie, staring excitedly at the monster truck. 'That lady had to use a ladder to get out!'

'Want me to run a check on the number plate, sir?' asked Agent K.

'If we find anything, we could arrest the driver,' added Agent T.

'No!' said Mrs Cook hastily. 'This is meant to be a peaceful holiday, remember?'

'Go for it!' growled Lara. 'Lock him up!'

Professor Cortex gave Lara a sympathetic look. 'I can guess what you're saying, GM451, but I'm afraid Mrs Cook has a point. You're supposed to be three perfectly ordinary pet dogs on holiday with their perfectly ordinary family. Ordinary families do not have Secret Service minders on hand to arrest anyone who happens to bother them.'

'That's decided then,' said Mrs Cook, yanking her suitcase from the car roof rack. 'Let's get on with our perfectly ordinary holiday, shall we?'

'We'll just check in,' said Mr Cook. 'No children or dogs allowed in this hotel, I'm afraid, so you lot will have to wait here. You're in charge, Lara.'

'No problem,' woofed Lara.

'And remember — act normal!' added Professor Cortex, hurrying after Mr and Mrs Cook.

'Normal? He can talk,' woofed Star, watching the professor's short white legs twinkle across the hotel car park as he tried to keep pace with his two black-suited bodyguards.

'No children or dogs?' Lara growled. 'What a cheek! We're much better behaved than some humans I could mention!' She raised an eyebrow and nodded towards the red monster truck.

Just then, the thin woman left the restaurant, carrying three pizza boxes. As she climbed up to the passenger side of the cab, the door swung open and a meaty hand emerged. Gratefully, the woman reached up, but the hand grabbed the boxes instead.

'I see what you mean, Ma,' said Spud, watching the woman scramble into the cab on her own. 'What a rude man.'

'You know, Agent K showed us how to run

a check on a car number plate,' said Ben thoughtfully.

'And I watched him type his log-in password,' added Sophie. 'It was KRACKERS.'

They both looked at Lara questioningly.

Lara hesitated. *Wait by the car. Act normal.* Those were her orders. On the other hand, it would be useful to know who the monster truck driver was, and where he lived, if only to make sure they didn't bump into him again. She nodded. 'OK,' she barked, waving them towards the Secret Service van. 'I'll keep a lookout for you.' She lifted a paw to shade her eyes and stared in the direction of the hotel.

Ben and Sophie hurried over to the van and climbed in. Lara squinted at the hotel entrance. *My eyesight isn't what it used to be*, she sighed. *I already need glasses for reading.* She thought about getting Sophie's birdwatching binoculars from the car, but decided that a binocular-wielding dog might attract too much attention.

'Spud and Star, you keep watch,' she barked, pointing at the hotel. 'I'll keep an eye on – OLLIE!!!'

While they had been talking, Ollie had

wandered off. He was standing beside the red monster truck, patting its huge wheels. As Lara raced towards Ollie, followed by Spud and Star, she imagined the big truck moving off and crushing him under its tyres. *And it would be my fault!* she panted, pushing herself to run faster. *I was meant to be watching him!*

She had nearly reached Ollie when the driver's window opened and someone threw out an empty pizza box.

'Hey!' Ollie yelled. 'You litter lout!' He bent to pick up the pizza box and an empty drinks can flew out of the window and hit him on the back of the head. A huge belch echoed from the cab.

'Owww!' Ollie straightened up and began to cry, rubbing his head where the can had hit it.

'Don't call me a litter lout, you crybaby!'

Lara, Spud and Star skidded to a stop beside Ollie and glared up at the window. A very fat man glared back at her. 'Children!' he sneered, chins wobbling. 'I hate them.'

'Looks like you've eaten one,' yelled Ollie through his tears.

'Oh dear!' wailed the thin woman, peering over the man's massive shoulder. 'Are you all right, little boy? I'm sure my son didn't mean to do that. Say sorry, Garry.'

'Gaz Guzzler never says sorry to anyone,' said the man.

'Why's she talking to him like he's Ollie's age?' asked Star. 'He must be at least twenty-five.'

'More like twenty-five tonnes!' growled Spud. 'Want me to karate-chop his nose, Ma?'

'No,' Lara woofed reluctantly. 'We're supposed to be acting like normal dogs, remember?'

As she turned to go, nudging Ollie ahead of her, a slice of half-chewed pizza flew from the window and hit her on the nose.

'Right. That's it! Forget normal!' Lara flipped the pizza slice in the air, caught it in her teeth and scrabbled up the side of the truck. The window began to slide shut, but Lara was too fast for it. She hooked her front paws over the top, stuck her head inside and slapped the pizza slice into Gaz's face.

'Ghaah!' he roared, scraping sauce from his cheeks and peeling two tomato slices from his eyes.

As Lara landed beside him again, Ollie stopped crying. 'Nice one, Lara!' he giggled, watching Gaz Guzzler pull strings of melted cheese out of his nose.

'We're not finished yet,' yapped Star. 'Come on, Spud!'

The two puppies scrambled up the side of the truck. They had trained on army assault

courses, climbing rope ladders as high as a house; scaling a monster truck was like a walk in the park to them.

'Hai-yah!' yelled Spud, thudding on to the bonnet.

'Time to practise some of those knots we learnt,' barked Star, landing beside him. She grabbed one of the truck's windscreen wipers

in her mouth and Spud grabbed the other. 'Ready, bro?' she asked, through a mouthful of wiper.

'Let's dance!' yapped Spud.

They yanked the rubber strips from the wipers and then began to twist and curve, jumping over and under one another. When they stopped a few seconds later, the windscreen wipers were tied together with a very professional double bow.

'You'll pay for this!' shouted Gaz.

'You'll have to catch us first,' yapped Spud.

'And I don't think you're fast enough,' added Star, blowing out her cheeks and waddling across the bonnet.

With a roar, Gaz Guzzler started the engine, the massive revs bouncing the puppies up and down. He crunched the monster truck into gear and sped off with Star and Spud still onboard. Quickly, they slid one to each side of the bonnet, hooked their paws over the wing mirrors and swung themselves down on to the door footrests. From there, they each did a swan dive from the truck, rolling as they hit the road and then coming up on to all four paws.

'Told you those gymnastics lessons would come in handy,' panted Star, winking at her brother. 'Wouldn't want to bump into him in a dark alley,' she woofed as they watched the monster truck career off down the street.

'It'd have to be a very wide alley!' replied Spud. 'Let's hope that's the last we see of "GUZZLER50".'

4. 'X' Marks the Spot

'This is more like it,' yapped Star, from one of three leather swivel chairs in the back of the Secret Service van. 'A girl deserves a bit of luxury sometimes, isn't that right, Ma?'

'Why only girls?' asked Spud, from the second swivel chair.

'Because we're worth it,' woofed Lara from the third chair, tossing her head like the girl in the shampoo advert.

Spud made a rude noise.

'Enjoy it while you can, Spud,' said Star. 'Tonight we're camping out in the forest!'

'That reminds me,' yapped Spud, nodding towards a padlocked trunk in the corner. 'I thought the prof got us into the van to show us his new gadgets?'

Lara looked at Professor Cortex, who was

sitting in the front of the van, chatting happily with Agents K and T. 'I think he just said that to get out of sitting next to Ollie in the car for the last part of the journey.'

'Good call,' laughed Star, pointing out of the back window at the Cooks' car. Ollie was bouncing up and down in his seat like a rubber ball.

'Shall we ask him to open it?' asked Spud, gazing curiously at the padlocked trunk.

'Not yet,' whispered Star, looking over her shoulder at Professor Cortex. 'First, *I* need to show you something.' She pawed at her collar and a tightly folded sheet of paper dropped into her lap. Quickly, she spread it out.

'What is it, sis?' asked Spud, leaning closer.

'It's the Gaz Guzzler info. Sophie slipped it under my collar outside the hotel.'

Lara balanced her reading glasses on her nose and together they scanned the page.

'Wow, look at that!' yapped Spud. 'He owns fifty different cars, trucks and bikes.'

'Fifty?' squeaked Star. 'He must have loads of money!'

'Pity he hasn't used it to buy himself some manners,' humphed Lara. 'What's his address?'

'Lakeside Mansion,' yapped Star. 'Now where have I seen that name before?' She raised her head and stared at the van monitor screens, which were all showing a map of the Clearwater Lake area. The forest where they were headed was shaded in red. On the lakeshore below the forest, there were two buildings close together — one was the Tall

Trees Outward Bound Centre and the other was Lakeside Mansion.

'Uh-oh,' sighed Star, pointing to Lakeside Mansion on the map. 'Meet Gaz Guzzler,' she woofed, slapping her paw against her forehead. 'Our next-door neighbour!'

As Lara, Star and Spud shared an annoyed glance, the van came to a halt. 'We're here!' cried Professor Cortex. 'Shake a leg, Spy Dogs — time to meet your trainer!'

'Oh well,' said Lara as they scrambled from their chairs. 'I doubt we'll bump into Gaz Guzzler again, even if he does live right next to the Outward Bound centre. I'm guessing he likes to drive everywhere, and we'll be hiking, climbing and canoeing.'

'And we'll make sure we don't go anywhere near Lakeside Mansion, won't we, Spud?' said Star.

Spud nodded his head furiously. 'Mmmfff!'

Star looked at her brother more closely. She spotted a corner of Sophie's computer printout sticking from the side of his mouth. 'What are you doing?'

Spud gulped, swallowed and then grinned at his sister. 'Eating the evidence!' he woofed.

'That's what spies do, you know – and I'm a Spy Dog.'

'You really do eat anything!' laughed Star.

Agent K opened the van doors and they jumped down into a forest clearing. The Cooks were climbing out of their car too. Ollie galloped off, riding an imaginary horse around the clearing. Spud bounded after him. He loved all the Cooks, but Ollie was his special friend and they often played together.

Star hurried over to Sophie and leant against her legs. 'This is where we say goodbye for a few days, Soph,' she woofed.

Sophie bent down and gave her a hug. 'Have a good time, Star. I'll miss you!'

'Not so fast, Sophie,' said Mrs Cook, folding her arms. 'I'm not leaving until I meet this mysterious Mr X.'

'Same here,' growled Lara. 'I don't leave my pups with just anyone.'

'I don't understand it,' said Professor Cortex. 'X said he would meet us here. Agents, search the area.'

Reluctantly, Agents K and T left the van. Agent K's face creased up in disgust as his foot squelched into a pile of poo. Agent T brushed against a tree trunk and then stared in horror at the green streak of moss on his sleeve.

'Not exactly outdoor types, are they?' commented Mr Cook.

'Yes, well, they don't get out of London much,' said Professor Cortex, blushing with embarrassment. 'Perhaps we should give them some help. Lara, Star and Spud, put your doggy senses to work.'

The three Spy Dogs spread out across the clearing and lifted their noses to the breeze.

'What do you smell?' asked Lara.

'Poo,' said Spud. 'Lots of poo. Deer poo, squirrel poo, bird poo –'

'That's enough poo,' interrupted Lara firmly. 'What about you, Star?'

'Leaves, mushrooms, rotting wood. No people, though, apart from our guys.'

'Spread out, team!' yapped Spud. 'We'll do a sweep.'

They sniffed their way forward, heads down. Star stuck her nose into a pile of dead leaves and then jumped backwards. 'Dog!' she barked. 'I smell dog!'

Two brown eyes opened in the pile of leaves.

Star gave a frightened yelp, but then one of the eyes winked at her.

'Well done, little one,' said a calm, friendly voice. 'You found me.'

The leaves parted and Star blinked. Suddenly, a majestic German Shepherd was sitting right in front of her.

'My name is Hero,' said the dog. 'You must be Star and Spud. Pleased to meet you both.'

'That was amazing!' yelped Star. 'I didn't

know you were there until I was nearly on top of you!'

'How did you hide so well?' barked Spud, running across to join Star.

'Camouflage,' said Hero, smiling at Lara over the heads of the pups. 'You'll be learning all about that over the next few days. For instance, if you roll in leaf mould, it makes it very hard for other dogs to scent you. Why don't you give it a go?'

Spud and Star began to roll around in the leaf mould, giggling as they did it. Lara relaxed and gave Hero a friendly nod. She could see that her pups were going to be in good hands. *Or should that be paws?*

'Aha!' Professor Cortex beamed. 'I recognize that dog! She belongs to X.'

'Excuse me!' woofed Hero, looking down her elegant nose at Professor Cortex. 'I don't *belong* to him. We're partners.'

'If she's here, then X can't be far away,' continued Professor Cortex. 'You can stop looking, agents!'

Gratefully, agents K and T abandoned their search and picked their way back to the van.

'Well they might be giving up,' barked

Hero, 'but I hope you two will keep looking.'

Eagerly, Spud and Star jumped up from the leaf mould.

'Is X really here?' asked Star.

'Yes,' said Hero. 'But he's in camouflage too.'

Spud looked around the clearing. All he could see were trees. 'This isn't going to be easy,' he sighed, leaning against the nearest trunk. A second later, he yelped and jumped away. The trunk had moved! He stared at the mossy bark and slowly he began to pick out a green and brown streaked face, half hidden under a green and brown balaclava.

'There he is!' yelped Spud, pointing at the tree. 'He's standing right there. X marks the spot!'

5. Honey, I Shrunk My Shorts

Everyone turned to look at the tree. The bark seemed to shiver and then a man stepped away from the trunk. He was dressed from head to toe in camouflage gear.

'Ah! There you are, X!' said Professor Cortex, shaking the survival expert by the hand. 'Very good camouflage! But how did you make sure the dogs wouldn't catch your scent?'

'Deer droppings,' said X. 'I mashed them up with my hands and then rubbed them all over.'

'Oh.' Professor Cortex yanked his hand out of X's grip and gave it a quick sniff. 'I smell – I mean, I see! Deer droppings, eh? Smell, smell, smell – I mean – well, well, well! You learn something new every day.'

'Speaking of days, there's not much of this one left,' said X, pointing at the afternoon sun.

'We should get going. Lots to do before dark.'

'Of course,' said Professor Cortex. 'I'll just demonstrate my latest gadgets and then we can all be on our way.'

'Are you heading back to London, Professor?' asked Mr Cook.

'No. My agents and I are staying nearby, at a top-secret base in the mountains. We're trying to train eagles to be airborne spies, but we're not having much luck. They keep getting distracted whenever they see a rabbit.'

While Professor Cortex hauled the trunk from the back of the van, Mrs Cook folded her arms and studied the survival expert.

'So, Mister ermm . . .?'

'X'

'So, Mister X. How long were you in the SAS?'

'I'm afraid that's classified information, ma'am,' said X.

'Very well. Then perhaps you can let me know how long you've been doing this sort of training?'

'Classified.'

'Hmmm,' frowned Mrs Cook. 'In that case, can you tell me —'

'Ma'am,' interrupted X, stepping forward and gazing deep into her eyes.

'Yes, Mister X?' said Mrs Cook, beginning to blush.

'You only need to know one thing, ma'am. While these pups are in my care, I will guard them with my *life*. With my *life*, ma'am. I promise.'

'Thank you, Mister X,' swooned Mrs Cook, putting a hand to her chest.

'Did you see that, Dad?' whispered Ben. 'He won Mum over just like that!'

'Must be some kind of hypnotist,' whispered Mr Cook out of the side of his mouth. 'It's taken me twenty years and I still haven't managed that!'

Professor Cortex opened the trunk. 'Gather round, everyone,' he called. 'I have three new gadgets for Star and Spud to test while they're here. First, two doggy scuba-diving suits.' He laid two puppy-shaped wetsuits on the ground, along with aqualungs, masks and flippers. 'There's even a tool belt, with specially adapted paw-grip tools. See?'

'Brilliant!' woofed Star. 'I can't wait to try those!'

'Me too!' yapped Spud, although secretly he was worried that his wetsuit might be a bit tight round the middle.

'Next, two new collar accessories. First, the Eazi-Freezi – a capsule that can freeze water instantly.' Professor Cortex held up two blue capsules and then bent to slot one each into the special compartments on Spud and Star's collars. 'Remember, pups, one press of the stud next to your collar buckle, and these compartments will spring open. Obviously not to be used while you're *in* the water; we don't want puppy-popsicles.'

Professor Cortex chuckled at his own joke, but then stopped when he peered over the top of his spectacles and saw no one else was laughing.

'Ahem. Moving on. Say you need to escape across a river. Chuck in the Eazi-Freezi capsule and you get an instant bridge! Or, when a baddie is after you, simply wait until he steps into some water, add one Eazi-Freezi capsule, and he's trapped in a block of ice!'

'Nice one,' yapped Star, patting her collar compartment.

'And last, but definitely not least,' said Professor Cortex proudly, 'the Big Squeeze.' He held up two little rubber balls on chains.

'They're not going to do much damage,' said Ben. 'They're only the size of marbles.'

'Ah, but it's what's inside them that counts,' said Professor Cortex, as he clipped the chains on to Spud and Star's collars. 'These little balls are packed with my special shrinking powder.

One good squeeze and the powder sprays out. *Pouff!*'

'Yes, but what does it "pouff"?' asked Sophie.

'Any man-made fibre,' said Professor Cortex. 'It won't shrink natural fibres, like wool or cotton, but nylon or Lycra will shrivel away to a tenth of its original size.'

'So, only useful if our baddie happens to be wearing a leotard,' woofed Star.

'If we find a ballet-dancing bank robber, we're in business,' added Spud.

'I know what you're thinking, pups,' said Professor Cortex. 'But man-made fibres are everywhere. With this shrinking powder, you could stop a criminal in his tracks. He can't run if his shoes have no soles! He can't drive away if his car seat has fallen apart! He can't call for a taxi if his mobile phone is the size of a postage stamp!'

'Brilliant!' said Sophie.

'Thank you, Sophie,' said Professor Cortex, straightening up and wiping his hands on his shorts. 'I must say I'm very proud of my shrinking pow . . . ow . . . OWW!' Professor Cortex stopped and looked down at his shorts, wondering why they were suddenly pinching his bottom. 'Oh no, I must've somehow picked up a trace of the powder on my hands!'

His shorts, which had been down to his knees, now looked like hot pants – and they were getting smaller by the second. Professor Cortex turned and ran, covering his bottom with his hands. By the time he reached the van,

his shorts were so tight he could not bend his legs to climb inside. Instead, he had to flop through the back door and shuffle in on his belly like a seal. Just before he disappeared from view, there was a high-pitched squeal as his shrinking shorts snapped up over his bum cheeks and became a thong.

Sophie looked alarmed. Ben stifled a giggle. Ollie laughed out loud. 'Cool,' he marvelled. 'The prof's got a wedgie!'

'Well,' woofed Spud, as the sound of wailing and ripping cloth echoed from the darkness of the van. 'At least we know it works.'

6. Kaboom!

Gaz Guzzler sat in his favourite armchair, chomping his way through a plate of deep-fried chicken legs. 'Are my cars washed?' he asked.

'Yes, sir, Mister Guzzler,' said Pete.

'Every single one?' demanded Gaz, pointing a greasy finger at Pete.

'All fifty of them,' said Pete, looking down at his own fingers, which were white and wrinkly after a day stuck in a bucket of hot water.

'Good. Tomorrow you can give them all a good wax and polish. That should keep you and your team busy until The Beast arrives tomorrow night. After that, you can get back to what I'm paying you for: Project Midas!'

After Pete had gone, Gaz settled back with

a satisfied grunt. 'Area of Outstanding Natural Beauty!' he snarled, glaring out of the window at the lake. 'What are they on about? There's nothing lovelier than gold – and nobody is going to stop me from getting more of it.'

He chuckled to himself. After months of trying, he had finally found a way to tunnel under their precious National Park without them suspecting a thing – and the entrance to his secret mine was so cleverly hidden, the chances were that no one would ever discover what he was up to.

'And if they do find out and put a stop to Project Midas, I've got a very nasty parting gift waiting for Clearwater Valley.'

Gaz hooked his finger under the gold chain round his neck and pulled a tiny gold box from inside his shirt. The box was a radio-controlled ignition switch; one press of the ruby set into the middle of it, and a timer would start ticking.

'Twenty minutes,' said Gaz, stroking his finger over the ruby. 'Just enough time for me to nip across the lake in my jet-ski and take off from the airfield in my private plane. Then – KABOOM!'

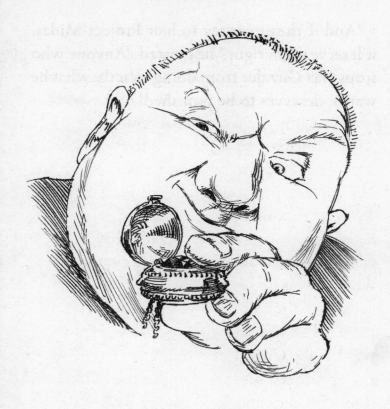

Nobody, not even Pete, knew about the bomb he had planted on the side of Clearwater dam. Gaz suspected that his mine foreman would have refused to do it, so he had squeezed into his mini-sub and done the job himself. He smiled as he imagined the dam blowing apart, releasing an avalanche of water on to the towns and villages below.

'And if they ever try to halt Project Midas, it'll serve them right,' he gloated. 'Anyone who stops Gaz Guzzler from doing exactly what he wants, deserves to be punished!'

7. *The Three Dinners*

This is the life! Lara thought.

She was sprawled in front of a log-burning stove, in the main room of the Tall Trees Outward Bound Centre. To one side of her, Sophie was snuggled up with a book. To the other side, Ben and Ollie were sitting together looking through the Tall Trees activities brochure.

'Wow! Abseiling!' said Ben.

'What's abs . . . ab . . . What's that sailing thingy?' asked Ollie.

'Not sailing. Abseiling. You climb down a cliff with a rope,' said Ben, showing Ollie the photograph in the brochure. 'I can't wait to try that.'

Ollie's eyes lit up. 'Me too!' he yelled.

'Well, I'm excited about canoeing over the sunken village,' said Sophie, looking up from her book. 'Imagine. A whole village at the bottom of the lake, with fish swimming in and out of the windows, and eels in the chimneys, and anemones in the gardens!'

Lara smiled to herself. Sophie had a good imagination.

'I wonder if you can see the houses down below?' said Ben.

'We'll ask Andrew when he comes back,' said Sophie.

Andrew, the friendly young owner of Tall Trees, was in the kitchen preparing their dinner. *He seems to do everything round here*, thought Lara. *Good job we're the only guests, or he'd be run off his feet!*

The smell drifting through from the kitchen made Lara's mouth water. She felt a pang of guilt as she remembered that Spud and Star were out in the forest, foraging for their supper. Spud had looked stricken when X had made him leave his food rucksack behind. He kept glancing sorrowfully back at it as he trailed into the forest after X, Hero and Star, with his tail between his legs.

Poor Spud, thought Lara. *But he could do with losing a few centimetres round his tum.*

'It's ready!' called Andrew from the kitchen.

They all raced for the big table in the middle of the room. Lara jumped up on to a chair, tied a napkin round her neck and picked up her knife and fork. When she looked up, she saw all three Cook children staring at her.

'What?' she woofed.

'You're meant to be an ordinary dog, remember?' hissed Ben.

Hastily, Lara dropped her knife and fork just before Andrew came in, carrying a big pot of stew.

'Haha!' laughed Andrew. 'Is your dog joining us?'

'Is that OK?' asked Sophie.

'Of course it is,' said Andrew, serving Lara with a generous portion of stew.

'She has very good table manners,' said Ollie. 'For a dog,' he added, as Lara began to tuck in with a loud slurping sound.

Cheek! Lara thought, giving Ollie a look. *You try eating this without a knife and fork. See how you get on!*

'So, what do you want to do tomorrow?' asked Andrew.

'Abseiling!' Ben and Ollie cried.

'No problem. What about you, Sophie?'

'Canoeing over the sunken village, please.'

Andrew's face fell. 'Sorry, Sophie. I'm afraid that activity is no longer available.'

'Why not?'

'Well, it's a bit of a long story. It all started when a man called Gaz Guzzler bought Lakeside Mansion, the big house just along the shore.'

The Cook children and Lara shared a look. *Gaz Guzzler again!*

'He thinks he can do anything he likes just because he's rich,' Andrew continued. 'He won the lottery seven years ago with the first ticket he ever bought, and since then, he's made loads more money mining for gold. He seems to have a knack for finding the stuff. Anyway, he moved here because he wanted to start mining in this valley.'

'There's gold here?' gasped Ollie. 'Right under our feet?'

'Gaz Guzzler thinks so,' said Andrew. 'But this is a National Park; you can't just walk in and start a big mining operation. Plus, this lake is actually a reservoir, so the water mustn't get polluted.'

'Ah! So that's why there's a village at the bottom of the lake,' said Sophie.

'Yes. When they built the dam, the valley flooded and the village got submerged.'

'So what happened about Gaz Guzzler's gold mine?' asked Ben.

'Lots of people objected to his plans, including me,' said Andrew. 'And the council told him he couldn't do it.'

Tantrum time, thought Lara, imagining Gaz Guzzler lying on the floor of the council chamber, drumming his heels and howling like a big baby.

'I bet he didn't like that!' said Ollie, echoing her thoughts.

'That's the odd thing,' said Andrew, looking puzzled. 'We all thought he'd kick up a big stink, but it's been months since the council told him he couldn't mine here, and there hasn't been a peep out of him.'

'I don't get it,' said Sophie. 'What's that got to do with us canoeing over the sunken village?'

'Well, unfortunately, the sunken village is right in front of his mansion. After I objected to his gold mine, he turned nasty. Whenever I took my guests canoeing or windsurfing on that part of the lake, he would chase us off on his jet-ski. The last thing you need when you're out in a canoe for the first time is a dirty great jet-ski roaring across your bows. I had to call a halt, for the safety of my guests.'

'So we can't go on the lake at all?' asked Ben.

'Yes, but only here, in front of the centre.' Andrew suddenly looked very sad. 'It's been so bad for business. I had to get rid of all my staff – and I'm not sure how much longer I can keep the place open on my own.'

So that's why we're the only guests, thought Lara.

'It's really unfair!' said Ben. Sophie and Ollie nodded their agreement.

Andrew shook himself. 'Enough gloom and doom!' he said, jumping up and collecting their plates. 'Ice cream and home-made apple pie coming up!'

Spud lifted his nose and sniffed the night air. He was sure he had just caught a whiff of apple pie. *Impossible!* he thought. *I'm in the middle of a dark, cold forest!* 'I'm hallucinating, sis,' he whimpered. 'It must be the lack of food.'

Star laughed as she pushed another branch into the sack X had given them. 'Don't be daft!' she said. 'You had a huge pile of sandwiches for lunch.'

'I know, but that was hours ago!' Spud's stomach rumbled and he groaned.

'Never mind,' said Star, taking pity on her brother. 'Look, our sack is full now. All we need to do is drag it back to camp. Come on, Spud, grab the other corner, and let's see what's for dinner!'

Spud's spirits lifted when they reached their campsite. X was stirring a billycan over a fire and delicious smells were drifting across the clearing. His mouth watered. 'Is it ready?' he yapped.

'Nearly,' woofed Hero. 'While we're waiting, bring your branches over to this fallen tree, and we'll build our shelter.'

Star's tail began to wag. She loved learning new things.

'What do you notice about the ground?' asked Hero.

'Dry and crumbly,' said Star, scratching at it with her paw.

'Exactly!' said Hero. 'Which makes it easy to dig.'

Spud groaned. 'We have to dig now?'

'That's right,' said Hero. 'We need to scoop out a sleeping area all along the sheltered side of the tree.'

They set to work and in no time they had dug out a long hollow.

'Next, we fill it with leaves,' said Hero.

'This is fun!' laughed Star, as she and Spud gathered up leaves and piled them into their bed. 'But why did we have to collect branches?'

'Every good shelter needs a rainproof roof,' explained Hero.

Together, they leant branches against the fallen tree to make a sloping roof. Then they added a layer of leaves before stacking the remaining branches on top.

'Brilliant!' said Star, crawling under the roof and snuggling down into their bed of leaves.

'Dry, warm and soft,' agreed Spud. 'We're proper survival experts, sis!'

'Come and get it!' called X.

This living off the land stuff isn't so bad after all, thought Spud as he bounded to the campfire where four tin plates had been set out. 'What's on the menu?' he yapped, trying not to dribble too much.

'These are made from wild buckwheat,' said X, putting a hot pancake on each plate.

Spud got ready to take a big bite of the pancake, but X ladled something else on to it from the billycan. It smelled delicious.

'This stew is a mixture of wild onions, wild mushrooms, bracken roots and dandelion leaves,' explained X. 'All easily found in the forest.'

Again, Spud got ready to take a big mouthful, but X still hadn't finished.

'And finally,' said the survival expert proudly, 'boiled beetle grubs!'

Spud gulped as he stared at the spoonful of

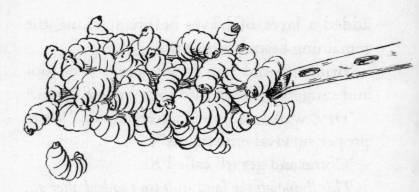

fat white grubs X had added to his plate. All of a sudden, he had lost his appetite. He glanced at Star. She was looking as sick as he felt.

'Dig in!' said X, shoving some of the glistening white bodies into his mouth. 'Grubs up!'

Mrs Cook was sitting in the hotel conservatory, eating her dinner from her lap. The food was delicious, but Mrs Cook hardly noticed the taste; she was much more interested in what she could see through her binoculars. Between forkfuls of food, she was watching the Tall Trees Outward Bound Centre on the other side of the lake.

Mr Cook was sitting on the next sunbed. His plate wobbled on his knees and he sighed as one of his sausages went skidding across the floor. 'Why don't we eat in the dining room? They've got proper tables and everything.'

'I'm sorry, dear, but after what happened on our last holiday, I'm determined to keep an eye on Ben, Sophie and Ollie.'

'It would be a real waste if you spent your whole holiday sitting here. What about trying some of the spa treatments tomorrow?'

'No, thanks. But you go ahead.'

Mr Cook gave up and settled down with a spa treatment booking form and a pen. He was keen to make the most of his free holiday. 'Now, let's see,' he muttered. 'Which treatments shall I book? Hmm. "Deep Muscle Massage". That sounds relaxing.' He ticked the massage box. 'And "Hydrotherapy". I'll have a go at that. What else? Oooh! Here's something called a "Full Body Wax". I wonder what that could be?' Mr Cook shrugged. 'Oh well, only one way to find out!' He ticked the box.

8. Over the Edge

Lara gazed into Ollie's eyes as he stood at the top of the cliff. She was looking for any hint of fear, but all she could see was excitement.

'Ready?' asked Andrew.

Ollie tightened his helmet strap and grinned. 'Ready!'

'OK,' said Andrew, gripping the safety rope. 'Off you go.'

Ollie leant back and stepped over the edge with a cry of 'Geronimo!'

Lara held her breath, but she need not have worried – Ollie abseiled down the cliff as though he had been doing it all his life.

'Well done!' shouted Andrew, as Ollie landed neatly at the bottom, where Ben and Sophie were waiting. They had both already done their first abseil.

'Can we do it again, please?' cried Ollie.

'Of course!' called Andrew. 'Ben and Sophie, can you help Ollie to unclip himself? Then just make your way back up the track. We'll be waiting for you, won't we, Lara?'

Lara woofed her agreement as she watched Andrew attach a new harness to the ropes. *I wish I could have a go*, she thought. *No, I mustn't! This weekend I'm just an ordinary family dog.*

She cocked her ears as an engine roared in the forest, shattering the peace. A second later, a quad bike burst on to the moor. The rider spotted Ben, Sophie and Ollie and changed direction. The quad bike roared up the slope, heading straight for them.

'Look out!' barked Lara.

Ben and Sophie were still unclipping Ollie from the rope. The quad bike bore down on them as they struggled to free him. Ben detached the final clip and they yanked Ollie out of the way just before the squat four-wheeler roared over the spot where they had been standing.

The rider turned his bike round and then raised his helmet visor, revealing podgy cheeks.

'Guzzler!' cried Andrew, dropping the abseiling harness and sprinting for the track that would take him down to the base of the cliff.

'Hey!' shouted Ben. 'You nearly ran us over!'

'Nearly? Oops. Sorry,' Gaz Guzzler said. 'I'll try to do better this time.'

He slammed down his visor, revved his engine and drove at them again.

Lara raced for the harness Andrew had dropped. Holding it between her teeth, she jumped over the edge of the cliff. The harness whizzed towards the ground, slowed only by the metal figure of eight the rope had to pass through. As Lara picked up speed, the rope began to swing, slamming her into the rock face. 'Oof! Ouch!' she yelped, using all four paws to push herself away again each time. *The world's first abseiling mutt!*

Ben, Sophie and Ollie flattened themselves against the cliff as the quad bike raced past, just missing their toes.

'Quick!' Sophie cried. 'Head for the track! He can't follow us up there.'

The three children began to run, but Gaz Guzzler was faster.

They're not going to make it! Lara thought. Quickly, she measured angles, speed and distance. When she hit the rock again, she pushed off as hard as she could and then let go of the harness. Paws waving, she fell through

the air and landed on top of Gaz Guzzler's
head.

'Umphh!' he gasped.

'Direct hit!' woofed Lara proudly.

The quad bike was still heading for Ben,

Sophie and Ollie. Lara hooked her back paws under Gaz's chin, stuck out her tail for balance and lunged for the handlebars. She managed to knock the quad off course just before it ploughed into the running children. Lara gave a sigh of relief. Her front paws lost their grip and she flopped down over the front of Gaz's helmet.

Suddenly, Gaz could see nothing through his visor except Lara's hairy belly. He slammed on the brakes, sending Lara sailing over his head. She hit the cliff and slid down to the ground.

'You again!' growled Gaz Guzzler, as his quad's engine spluttered to a stop. 'Pesky dog!'

'Lara!' cried Ben, kneeling beside her. 'Are you all right?'

'Never better,' croaked Lara, staggering to her feet.

Ben gave her a fierce hug, squeezing her bruised ribs.

'Ow,' yelped Lara. 'Ow. Ow.' But she didn't stop him.

'What do you think you're doing, Guzzler?' yelled Andrew, reappearing at the bottom of the track.

'Making your guests feel unwelcome, of course,' said Gaz.

'You big bully!' shouted Andrew. 'Pick on someone your own size!'

That might be difficult, thought Lara, eyeing Gaz Guzzler's enormous belly.

'If you have a problem with me, then you take it out on me,' continued Andrew. 'Not them!'

'Oh, but I am taking it out on you,' said Gaz with a cold smile. 'If I get rid of all your guests, you'll have to close down Tall Trees for good.'

'All this because Andrew stopped you from opening one more gold mine?' asked Sophie.

'Who says he stopped me? You just wait! After tonight –' Gaz stopped. Suddenly, he looked shifty, as though he had said too much.

'Tonight? What's happening tonight?' asked Ben.

'None of your beeswax,' said Gaz.

'Cooo-eee!'

Everyone turned round to see a thin, worried-looking woman running up the hillside towards them, carrying a rucksack.

'Give me that,' said Gaz, grabbing the rucksack from his mother and pulling out a triple-decker meatball sandwich.

'Is something wrong?' panted Mrs Guzzler, holding her aching sides as she looked round at the circle of unhappy faces.

Gaz was too busy chomping to answer her, so Ollie piped up instead. 'He nearly ran us over with his quad bike!'

'Oh dear. I'm sure he didn't mean to,' said Mrs Guzzler. 'But you do drive your quad a bit too quickly, Garry. I couldn't keep up with you, and I was running as fast as I could. Say sorry, son.'

Gaz gave a snort, spraying chewed-up meatballs all over Ollie. Then he started his quad and set off down the hillside.

'There! All sorted,' said Mrs Guzzler brightly, patting Ollie on the head.

'That wasn't an apology,' protested Ben, but Mrs Guzzler was already sprinting away after the quad bike.

'Don't mind Garry,' she called over her shoulder. 'He's a good boy, really.'

'Good for nothing' growled Lara. She hated baddies and Gaz Guzzler was as bad as they came.

9. The Beast Arrives

That night, Spud lay awake at one end of the sleeping shelter. Next to him, Star was twitching in her dreams. Next to her, Hero was curled up with her tail over her nose and, at the other end of the sleeping hollow, X snored softly.

Flubbalubbalubbahh, gurgled Spud's stomach.

'That's why I can't sleep – because I'm so hungry!' he whined. He stared up at the roof of the shelter. The branches reminded him of breadsticks and the dead leaves looked like cheese and onion crisps. Quickly, he closed his eyes and thought about the day instead. They had learnt how to hide, follow a trail and signal for help. X had helped the puppies to spell 'SOS' in a clearing. 'It's an emergency signal,' he'd explained. But all Spud could think of was that 'SOS' was short for 'sausages'!

FLUBBALUBBALUBBLE! rumbled Spud's stomach, as soon as he thought of sausages.

'That's it!' he muttered, clutching his belly. 'I have to find something to eat – and I know just where to go!'

He eased out of the sleeping shelter, tiptoed across the clearing and hurried downhill. He was aiming for the Tall Trees centre, where he planned to sneak into the kitchen for a quick midnight feast.

A white fog was rising from the lake when Spud stepped from the forest on to the shore. He peered around, trying to work out where he was. To his right, he could just make out the high boundary wall of Lakeside Mansion.

'Evening, Boss,' said a man's voice from the other side of the wall. 'When will the beast arrive?'

The puppy shrank into the shadows, his heart beating fast. *A beast?*

'Any minute now,' said the voice of Gaz Guzzler. 'I expect you to have it settled in before the end of the night. Is that clear?'

Spud frowned. What was Gaz Guzzler up to? He waited, but everything was quiet again, except for his rumbling stomach, which got louder and louder. He shrugged, turned to his left and headed for Tall Trees. His mouth watered as he imagined the treats waiting for him in the kitchen. *Priorities*, he thought. *I must find food first and sort the beast out later.*

Spud stopped when he heard a swishing noise coming from the lake behind him. He turned round and gave a gasp of horror as a huge beast loomed out of the mist. It had a long neck and two red eyes that were glaring straight at him!

Spud stood frozen to the spot, too scared to run as the beast glided across the water. Soon it would be close enough to bend its long neck down to the shore and swallow him up in one gulp.

Spud's short life passed before him. 'Goodbye, Ma. Goodbye, Star. Goodbye, Ben, Sophie and Ollie!' he whimpered, closing his eyes. *I'm about to be eaten by the Loch Ness Monster!*

The swishing sound stopped. Spud opened one eye. The beast had come to a halt in front of Lakeside Mansion. He held his breath, waiting to see what it would do next. The beast glared at him for a few more seconds before

sinking beneath the waves with a mournful sigh. The surface of the lake bubbled and hissed, and then everything was calm again.

Spud let out his breath. All thoughts of food had left his mind. Slowly, he backed towards the forest, not daring to take his eyes off the lake until he had reached the safety of the trees. Only when he could hear leaves rustling above his head, did he turn round and race all the way back to camp with his tail between his legs.

10. Dogfish

'I'm telling you, sis, I saw a monster last night!'

Star laughed. 'Pull the other one!'

Spud scowled. He had been waiting all morning to be alone with Star so that he could tell her about his scary encounter, and now she didn't believe him!

'Come on,' said Star, trotting off through the forest. 'Hero and X are way ahead of us.'

'I'm not joking!' cried Spud, hurrying to catch up with her. 'It was as big as a house, and it had a long neck and red eyes. Just like Nessie!'

Star shook her head. 'Don't be silly. The Loch Ness Monster isn't real.'

'How do you know?' Spud demanded.

'Because they've searched Loch Ness from top to bottom. If there was a monster in there, they would've found it.'

'Well, maybe they should come and search Clearwater Lake instead! There's a monster in there, and it's got something to do with Gaz Guzzler.'

Star stopped and looked at her brother. 'You're serious, aren't you?'

'I've never been more serious in my life!'

Star hesitated. 'Spud, when I woke up this morning, you were whimpering in your sleep. It sounded as though you were having a nightmare –'

'That monster wasn't a nightmare! It was real!'

'Are you sure?'

'Well . . . It *felt* real,' said Spud, but he was beginning to wonder whether he had dreamt the whole thing.

'You always have nightmares when you go to bed hungry,' Star reminded him.

Spud nodded. 'You're right. And my tum was very empty last night. Phew! It *was* just a dream. Thanks, sis.' He gave a relieved laugh and pushed Star over. 'What're you lying down there for?' he yapped, running after Hero and X.

'Spud!' shouted Star. 'Wait till I catch you!'

Spud was still laughing when he burst out of the forest, but he soon stopped when he saw where he was. In front of him, the lake gleamed in the morning sun, and Hero and X were standing on the shore with Professor Cortex's doggy diving suits laid out at their feet.

'It's a lovely morning for a swim,' said X.

Spud gulped.

'It was only a dream, remember,' whispered Star, trotting past him down to the shore.

'Only a dream,' Spud repeated under his breath as he squeezed into his wetsuit, mask and flippers. 'No monsters in this lake.'

'Now, don't stay under for too long,' said X, as he checked their oxygen cylinders. 'The lake water is very cold at this time of year, and we don't want you getting hypothermia.'

'Hypo-whatia?' yapped Star.

'Hypothermia,' barked Hero. 'It's when you get too cold. It can be fatal.'

Spud cast a nervous glance at his sister. *Monsters and hyper-whatsit*, he thought. *Not sure I fancy this!*

But Star was wagging hard as she pulled on her scuba gear.

'OK, pups,' said X. 'Just try a five-minute dive to test the equipment.'

Spud's heart was beating fast as he flapped his flippered paws down to the water's edge. He and Star paddled out and ducked under the surface. To start with, he tried to look everywhere at once, but soon he forgot all about monsters. It was beautiful under the water. Bright green weeds swayed, and hundreds of fish darted about. Crabs skittered across the bottom and an eel trailed through the water like a long brown ribbon.

All was quiet too, except for the sound of bubbles and doggy breathing.

When Star pointed upwards and began to

swim for the surface, Spud followed reluctantly. He couldn't believe that their five minutes were up. The time had flown by.

'That was amazing!' he yapped, spitting out his mouthpiece as soon as he surfaced.

'I know!' woofed Star, turning to wave to Hero and X. Her eyes widened with excitement when she saw an otter looking at her. It was lying on its back in the water, eating mussels.

Star paddled over. 'Hello,' she said, in her best Otterese.

'What are you two? A pair of dogfish?' The otter chuckled to himself and cracked open another mussel.

'You live in a lovely lake,' said Star.

'Thank you. Most of it's all right,' said the otter. 'But I'm not so keen on that bit round the bend.'

'Which bit?' asked Star.

'The part in front of the big house. Stay away from there, little dogfish.'

Star felt a cold chill run down her back under the wetsuit. 'Why? What's there?' she asked.

'A village, under the waves,' said the otter. 'We used to play there, but not now. It's haunted.'

Star shuddered. 'Haunted?'

'Yes. Strange things live there. Strange lights shine from the houses. And, last night, a beast arrived.'

'A beast?' squeaked Star, but the otter had finished eating its mussels.

'Gotta go. Bye-bye, little dogfish!' it cried, disappearing with a flip of its tail.

'You look worried, sis,' said Spud. 'What did the otter say?'

Star swallowed. The monster could be lurking under her paws right now! 'Um, you know that dream you had?'

'Ye-es,' said Spud, watching her face.

'Well, it might not have been a dream after all,' whispered Star.

'What!' yelped Spud.

'That otter saw a monster last night too. In the lake in front of Gaz Guzzler's mansion.'

'Exactly where I saw it!'

'The otter said there's a haunted village down there.'

'H-h-haunted?'

The two pups stared at one another.

'Let's get out of here,' gasped Spud, breaking into front crawl.

Star turned and breaststroked for the shore as fast as her short legs would go.

'You know what I think?' said Star as they

scrambled out of the water. 'I think we've got a mystery to solve.'

Spud nodded. He stood proudly and puffed out his chest. 'We are Spy Dogs, after all. And we know how to use our scuba-diving suits now. How about we pay that haunted village a little visit tonight?'

'It's a deal, bro,' yapped Star.

11. 'What Could Possibly Go Wrong?'

'Ready?' asked Andrew.

Ben, Sophie and Ollie gripped the bars of their windsurfer sails. 'Ready!' they cried.

'Off you go!' yelled Andrew.

Together, they hauled up the sails, bent their knees and leant backwards. Their sails caught the wind and they surfed across the water in a wobbly line.

'Yay! We're doing it!' yelled Ollie. 'Look, Lara, we're windsurfing! Oops.' Ollie's sail flapped and jumped out of his hands. He tried to stay on his board, but lost his balance, fell off and disappeared under the water.

Lara stood up and took a step towards the lake, but Ollie quickly resurfaced, whooping with laughter. Ben fell off next, then Sophie.

They waded to the shore together, dragging their boards behind them.

'Well done, you three!' said Andrew, pulling the boards up above the water line. 'You managed to do some proper windsurfing after just one lesson; that's pretty impressive. Did you enjoy it?'

'It was brilliant!' said Sophie.

'Can we do some more?' asked Ben.

'Tomorrow,' said Andrew. 'The lake's getting a bit cold now. Why don't you have a rest, while I go and get the dinner ready?'

'OK,' said Ollie. 'Can we stay by the lake, though?'

'As long as you get out of those wetsuits and into some warm clothes. And you must promise not to go out on the boards on your own.'

'We promise,' chorused Ben, Sophie and Ollie.

I didn't promise, thought Lara, as Andrew left. She raised a paw to her eyes and scanned the lake. *Nobody about but us. I'll just have a quick session while the children are getting changed.*

When Ben looked up a few minutes later, he saw Lara whizzing across the water on a surfboard with the wind whistling through the bullet hole in her sticky-up ear.

Woohoo!

Mrs Cook had her binoculars trained on the windsurfing lesson. 'Lifejackets? Check. Helmets? Check. Staying in shallow water? Check.' She gave a satisfied nod. 'Oh, look! Lara's having a go now! They all seem to be having a lovely time.'

'I wish I was,' groaned Mr Cook, hobbling into the hotel conservatory.

Mrs Cook put down her binoculars and turned to look at her husband. He was wearing a spa robe and his bare legs were as red as boiled lobsters. 'My goodness!' she gasped. 'What happened to you?'

'I signed up for a full body wax,' winced Mr Cook. 'I thought it sounded rather nice. But it wasn't. It was very painful!'

'Yes, I can imagine,' said Mrs Cook sympathetically. Mr Cook had always been proud of his hairy chest, but she could see that it was now as hairless and pink as a baby's bottom.

'Before the body wax,' moaned Mr Cook, 'I had some hydrotherapy, which I thought would be a nice, relaxing bath. Instead, they stood me against a wall and hosed me down with icy water.' He shuddered. 'And then I had a deep-muscle massage, which was . . .' Mr Cook closed his eyes and tried to blot out the memory of being bent into the shape of a pretzel by a man who would not have looked out of place in a World Wrestling Federation ring.

'Come on,' said Mrs Cook, getting to her feet. 'I'll choose the spa treatments from now on.'

'You mean, you're going to come to the spa with me?' said Mr Cook, brightening.

'Yes, I am. You're absolutely right, dear – it's a waste of a holiday if I spend it stuck in here. Besides, they're all having such a good time over there; what could possibly go wrong?'

12. The Haunted Village

A full moon was riding high in the sky as Star and Spud slipped into the water and began to swim to the bottom of the lake. Moonlight lit their way at first, but soon the water was so dark, they had to switch on their headlamps.

The deeper they went, the colder the water became. Star began to shiver. She looked across at Spud, but the freezing water seemed to be having no effect on him. *It can't be much further*, she thought, feeling the tip of her tail turn to ice. *This is a mission. I'll just grit my teeth and keep going*. A few seconds later, Spud nudged her and pointed. Star squinted through her mask and saw some pale yellow lights directly ahead. They were shining from the glassless windows of a group of ruined cottages.

The haunted village! Star turned off her

headlamp and ducked behind a tumbled drystone wall. Spud joined her there and they gazed at the village. The cottages were clustered round what would once have been the village green. A church stood in one corner, with its stone tower pointing the way to the surface.

Star began to shiver even more. She was now scared as well as cold. How could lights be glowing in the windows of an underwater village? She had never believed in ghosts, but she was beginning to think she might have been wrong.

Well, at least there's no sign of Spud's monster, she thought, but a second later, Spud jabbed her in the ribs and pointed at the church tower. Star could not believe her eyes! Something was rising out of the top of the tower. It had two red eyes and a long neck. *The monster!* It had been hiding in the tower and now it was coming out to get them!

The great beast rose up higher and higher until it towered over Star and Spud. They clutched at one another and shrank down behind the ruined stone wall. There was no point in trying to escape; they knew that as soon as they moved, the beast would see them.

All they could do was stay where they were and keep as still as statues.

Star was quivering like a jellyfish. She could hear her breathing magnified in the swimming mask. Finally, she could bear the suspense no longer. The puppy raised her head and stared at the creature. She saw five white letters stretching down the monster's long neck. The letters spelled out B.E.A.S.T. Star frowned and looked more closely. Each letter was the start of a word!

Bio
Engineered
Air
Supply
Tower

Star gave a gasp of relief. The B.E.A.S.T. was not a monster at all — it was a machine! The long neck was a steel tower. The red eyes were lights. She tapped Spud on the shoulder and then bent down and wrote in the sand.

It's a machine!

Just then, the B.E.A.S.T. gave a low moan and began to sink slowly back down into the church tower. *It's pumping air into something*, thought Star. *But what? Time to find out what Gaz Guzzler is up to.*

Star pointed at the church and Spud nodded. They were about to break cover when a frogman swam out of the church, guiding a motorized underwater sledge in front of him. He disappeared into one of the cottages.

Spud looked at her and shrugged. Star knew what he was asking. *What do we check out first?* She pointed at the church and they set off together, keeping as low as they could and using rocks and weeds for cover. Inside the church, instead of pews and an altar, they saw a huge circular door made of reinforced steel. The sign on the door read: CAUTION! MAKE SURE THE INNER DOOR IS SEALED BEFORE OPENING THE OUTER AIRLOCK DOOR!

That frogman must've come out of there, thought Star. *But what was on the motorized sledge — and where was he taking it?*

Spud beckoned her out of the church and they set off for the cottage where the frogman had disappeared. Star was kicking her flippers as fast as she could, but she was having trouble keeping up with her brother. Her heart was thumping and her sight kept blurring. She tapped her oxygen gauge. *Everything seems fine. But why do I feel so drowsy?*

Spud reached the cottage and peered in through the window. Inside, there was a bank of screens, switches and winking lights, but there was no sign of the frogman. He read the words flashing up on the screens. Airlock Sealed. Drilling in progress. B.E.A.S.T. air filters operating. He frowned and tried to think. The words were telling him something about what Gaz Guzzler was up to, but he couldn't quite put the clues together. His mind felt slow and stupid, and he realized he was shivering. Spud turned to his sister. *She's the clever one. Maybe Star knows what those words mean.*

But Star was nowhere to be seen. Spud was frantic. He twirled a full 360 degrees and peered into the blackness. Another frogman flipped by and he sank into the dark water. *Sis, where are you?* he thought. *Captured? Injured?* His body shuddered. *Or worse?* Spud's mind was numb with cold. There was only one thing he could do and he knew it was risky. The puppy switched on his lamp and swam frantically through the village. *Nothing! Come on, sis, give me a clue!* Spud's torch caught sight of some bubbles rising from the bottom of the lake. He focused his torch towards the source and caught a flash of something white. The brave puppy pumped his short legs and delved deeper into the water. His torch picked out the lifeless body of his sister lying in the silt at the bottom of the lake. 'No way!' he barked through his mouthpiece. Star's eyes were glazed, but there were bubbles coming from

her mask so Spud hoped for the best. He grabbed his sister's collar and pulled. *Crikey, I thought I was the heavy one!* Spud knew there wasn't much time. His sister's body was stone cold and the needle on his oxygen tank was in the red zone. He was about to swim for the surface when a group of frogmen emerged from the church and headed straight towards him. Quickly, he turned off his torch and tugged Star into the cottage with the bank of screens.

As he ducked behind the screens, he saw a dark tunnel entrance cut into the floor of the cottage. Dragging his sister behind him, Spud swam into the tunnel, his legs pumping furiously. *Yes! We're in luck!* he thought as he saw a circle of light above their heads. *We might just get out of this alive!* A second later, his oxygen alarm started beeping. 'Not now!' he grunted as he shook off his oxygen cylinder and let it fall to the tunnel floor. Now with less weight, but just one lungful of oxygen left, he kicked upwards through the tunnel, towards the circle of light above their heads. Spud's eyes started bulging and he was getting dizzy, but he held on to his sister's collar and continued kicking.

He was so proud to be a Spy Pup. He'd either save his sister or die trying. The light was getting closer. *But it's so slow. This is my moment*, thought the puppy. *This is what Spy Dogs do!* Spud spluttered to the surface, gorging himself on lungfuls of air. He dragged his lifeless sister towards a platform and tugged her to safety. Spud took out Star's mouthpiece and removed her oxygen tank. He lay her on her front in the recovery position and pumped her back like he'd seen someone do in a movie. *Come on, sis*, he urged. *We're a team!* After a while he heard Star groan. Her eyes flickered open and Spud kept pumping. 'What are you doing, stupid,' coughed his sister. 'Are you trying to kill me?'

Spud looked crestfallen. 'Well, the exact opposite, actually,' he complained. 'I thought you might have swallowed some water.'

'I'm just f-f-frozen,' explained Star through chattering teeth. 'Chuck me a t-t-towel and I'll be fine.'

Spud reached for a fluffy towel from the row of wetsuits and towels hanging up to dry, and wrapped his sister up. She looked cute with her nose poking out, the chattering teeth muffled by the towel.

The pups surveyed the scene. They were in an underground chamber with arc lights strung from the ceiling.

There was a stone platform along the far wall of the chamber. Concrete stairs climbed from the platform to a door set in the wall. 'I bet that door goes into Gaz Guzzler's mansion,' whispered Spud excitedly.

Star tried to answer, but her mouth wouldn't work. She had stopped shivering at last, but

her head felt as big and empty as a balloon. *I think I need a little nap*, she thought, closing her eyes.

A frogman surfaced and hauled himself on to the platform. The puppies disappeared under the towel, hidden except for peeping eyes. Two men appeared from the doorway and heaved an underwater sled on to the concrete platform. It looked very heavy. Star held her jaw shut with her paw to stop her teeth chattering. One

of the men lifted a gleaming lump of gold from the sled and held it up to the light. 'Mister Guzzler will be pleased!' he said.

'Look at that, sis!' whispered Spud. 'It's gold! Gaz Guzzler is mining for gold under the lake, where nobody can see what he's up to!'

Star did not answer. Spud turned to look at his sister. Her eyes were closed and her head was lolling to one side. 'Star!' he hissed, grabbing her by the shoulders, 'this is no time for a snooze.' But Star had no choice. She'd used up her energy reserves and her body had shut down.

Spud cuddled up to Star and wrapped the towel round them both. He held her tight, giving her the warmth of his body and willing her to wake up. After a long time, he laid his cheek next to hers and began to cry silent tears. He was lost in an underground cave, surrounded by baddies. *I'm only a pup*, he sobbed. *I'm not ready for this!*

Star woke Spud with a big wet lick. 'Come on, bro,' she whimpered. 'Time to solve this crime!'

Spud shook himself awake and his wag

kicked in. 'Thought you were a goner for a minute, sis,' he admitted. 'What happened?'

'Hypothermia,' yapped Star. 'But you saved me, bro!'

'How come I didn't get it?' asked Spud, squinting up at his sister.

'Padding,' said Star, patting his tum. 'Nothing like a nice layer of fat to keep you warm. Sometimes it pays to be podgy!'

Spud wagged harder. His tummy rumbled. 'Time to find our way out of this cave,' he yapped. 'And maybe we can find some food on the way!'

The puppies waited until the coast was clear before creeping out from their snuggly hiding place. The door was slightly ajar and the tiny dogs disappeared into the crack. 'Too easy,' woofed Star as the pair scampered up a flight of stairs and through another door. They found themselves in Gaz Guzzler's kitchen, the shelves groaning under the weight of sausages and pies. A small army of staff scurried around, preparing Gaz's huge meals. Star went first, darting between the feet of a chef and out through the back door. Spud wanted to follow, but his nose wouldn't let him. *Sausages*, he sniffed. *Fried. With bacon and eggs! Mmmm!*

Star stood at the door and beckoned to her brother. *Come on, Spud*, she urged, waving her paws. *We have to get back and tell X all about it!*

Spud's head knew his sister was right. But his stomach was boss. 'Geronimooo,' he woofed as he leapt from his hiding place on to the kitchen table. A lady screamed and a frying pan fell to the floor. 'Perfect!' woofed Spud as he leapt at the bread bin and grabbed two slices of Gaz's best white sliced. 'Maximum chaos! Sausages next,' he whooped as he slid from the table and nuzzled a couple off the floor. *Ouch, hot!* He managed a quick squirt of tomato sauce before he disappeared out of the back door to join his sister.

The pair eventually stopped running when they reached the forest. The puppies sat, panting, their tongues lolling. Spud proudly handed his sister a sausage sandwich and the pair munched happily. Spud wagged extra hard as he gobbled his breakfast. 'Do you know what, sis?' he slurped. 'This could be our best mission ever!'

13. Proof!

Energy restored, the puppies galloped to the camp.

'Where are X and Hero?' woofed Star, looking around their sleeping shelter.

'Gone,' said Spud.

'But we have to tell them about Gaz Guzzler and the underwater gold mine!'

'We'll have to find them first,' said Spud, dropping a sheet of paper on to the leaves. It was a note from X.

'Aww, look! Signed with a kiss,' joked Star. 'I think he's starting to like us.'

'Do you think he'll believe us?' asked Spud as they set off through the forest with their noses to the ground.

'I hope so,' said Star. 'But I wish we had some proof. A photograph of the B.E.A.S.T.

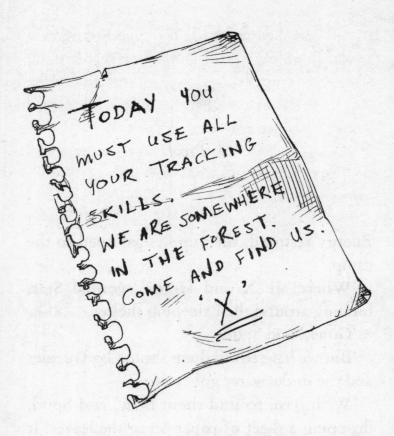

TODAY YOU MUST USE ALL YOUR TRACKING SKILLS. WE ARE SOMEWHERE IN THE FOREST. COME AND FIND US.

'X'

or a piece of mining equipment, or something.'

'Sorry, sis,' said Spud. 'I didn't have time to take any holiday snaps. I was too busy saving your life!'

Star rolled her eyes at her brother. 'Get tracking, big-head.'

X and Hero were very good at covering their tracks, but every now and then Spud and Star

102

found a broken cobweb, a snapped twig, or a paw print. Slowly, they moved on through the trees, so wrapped up in the hunt that they forgot about everything else until they heard a familiar voice ring out.

'Hurry up, Pete! My breakfast's getting cold!'

'Gaz Guzzler!' whispered Spud.

'And he sounds close!' Star replied.

The two pups raised their heads and looked about them. The boundary wall of Lakeside Mansion was at the bottom of the slope. They could see over the wall to the shore of the lake where Gaz Guzzler and Pete were standing together.

Spud and Star crept closer to watch the two men.

'I've got something better than breakfast to show you, Boss,' said Pete, reaching into his pocket.

'I doubt it,' snapped Gaz.

Pete pulled out a lump of gold.

Gaz's eyes gleamed greedily. He grabbed the gold and cradled it in his hand. 'Lovely,' he breathed. 'You'll all get a bonus in your pay packets this week.'

'Thanks, Boss!'

'Now go and get me more gold, Pete. Lots more!'

The foreman hurried off and Gaz stood on the shore, stroking the gold with his fat fingers.

'You know what I'm thinking?' whispered Star.

'Proof!' hissed Spud.

The two pups balanced across a fallen tree to the top of the boundary wall and then jumped down into a handy bush. Swiftly, silently, they made their way through the mansion grounds to the lake shore.

Gaz Guzzler stuffed the gold into the pocket of his tracksuit bottoms and began to waddle back to the house.

'Quick!' hissed Star. 'We've only got a moment. You spray him. I'll grab the gold. Then we run for it!'

Spud jumped out in front of Gaz. 'Hai-yah!' he yapped, striking a karate pose.

'I don't know where you came from,' growled Gaz, scowling down at the plump black puppy at his feet. 'But I know where you're going. In the lake!'

As Gaz reached for him, Spud grabbed the little rubber ball hanging from his collar and bit down on it. A white powder puffed out of the ball, settling all over Gaz Guzzler's clothes.

Spud turned to run, but he was too slow. He was caught by the scruff of the neck and lifted into the air.

'Pesky pup!' growled Gaz. He pulled his arm back to throw Spud into the lake, but stopped short when his football shirt split down the front. He stared at his huge white belly in surprise. 'How did that happen?'

The shirt shrivelled away into a tiny vest, then that tore too. Next, his tracksuit bottoms began to slip down over his enormous bum.

'Ooooh!' shrieked Gaz, trying to hold his trousers up with his other hand. It was no good. The lump of gold fell out of his pocket as his trousers shrank down to his thighs, split in half and turned into a pair of tight black stockings. As the stockings ripped into fishnets and then fell away, Star ran out and grabbed the gold between her teeth.

'Eeek!' howled Gaz as his trainers folded up round his massive feet. His toes burst out of the front, his heels ballooned out of the back and then his trainers exploded with a loud *POP*! Gaz was left wearing nothing but a pair of white cotton Y-fronts and a pair of laces.

'What . . .? What . . .? What just happened?' he stuttered.

'Put me down!' yapped Spud, trying to squirm out of Gaz's grip.

Gaz gripped him harder, making him yelp. 'You did this,' he hissed, glaring at Spud. 'But how? And why? Where's your owner?'

'Let go of him!' barked Star, shifting the lump of gold to the side of her mouth.

Gaz jumped and looked down at the little black and white puppy with the sticky-up ear. 'Another one?' he growled. 'And what's that in your mouth?' His eyes widened. 'My gold!' he roared. 'Give it back!'

Star shook her head. 'Let Spud go first,' she woofed.

'You'd better drop that right now,' yelled Gaz. 'Or I'll hurt your little friend. Understand?'

Star hesitated. She looked at her half-choked brother. This had not been part of the plan!

14. Captured

Lara lay back in the stern of the canoe and crossed her legs. *I could get used to being a lady of leisure*, she thought, letting one paw flop over the side to trail in the water. Andrew was sitting in front of her, paddling with hardly a ripple. Ollie was in the bows, trying to copy him.

He's doing very well, thought Lara kindly as Ollie slapped the water with his paddle, sending another fountain shooting up into the air.

Ben and Sophie were paddling a second canoe alongside them. Nobody was talking, but everyone was smiling, enchanted by the beauty and stillness of the lake. They paddled in peaceful silence from one end of the bay to the other. There, Andrew brought his canoe round in front of Ben and Sophie.

'Sorry, folks,' he said reluctantly. 'We have to turn back here. Gaz Guzzler's mansion is just round the bend.'

'That's a shame,' sighed Ben. 'I think I could paddle this canoe forever.'

'It's so peaceful, isn't it, Lara?' murmured Sophie.

Lara was about to wag her agreement when a dreadful, high-pitched yelp shattered the silence. It was the sound of a puppy in pain, and it was coming from Lakeside Mansion.

'Spud!' yelped Lara, scrambling to her paws. Without a second thought, she threw herself into the water and started swimming.

'Come on, Sophie!' cried Ben, jamming his paddle into the water. Sophie did the same and their canoe shot past Andrew, heading for Gaz Guzzler's mansion.

'Stop!' shouted Andrew.

'No! Go!' Ollie yelled. 'Spud needs help!'

'Who's Spud?' Andrew demanded, paddling after Lara, Ben and Sophie.

'That's Spud,' said Ollie as they rounded the bend.

Andrew blinked. A sumo wrestler was

standing on the shore in front of Lakeside Mansion, wearing a tiny white nappy and holding a small black puppy by the scruff of the neck. Another puppy, this one black and white, was barking up at the sumo wrestler.

'Put him down!' yelled Ollie.

The sumo wrestler bent and grabbed the other puppy by the scruff of the neck. 'Nothing to see here!' he shouted, holding both pups up

in front of his nipples like a furry bra. 'Turn round and paddle away!'

'Hang on,' said Andrew, rubbing his forehead. 'That's not a sumo wrestler. That's Gaz Guzzler in some very skimpy underpants. What's going on?'

'Tell you later,' Ben promised. 'Just help us get our pups back, please?'

The two canoes and Lara arrived on the shore at the same time. Lara shook herself and then

stalked up the beach towards Gaz, growling menacingly. Ben, Sophie, Ollie and Andrew hurried after her.

'Are you all right, pups?' woofed Lara.

'Oh, not bad, Ma,' winced Spud, as Gaz took a firmer hold on his scruff. 'We're just, you know, hanging around.'

'I said there's nothing to see here,' said Gaz Guzzler. 'And you're trespassing. Get off my land!'

'Not until you give us our puppies,' said Ben.

'Call off that ugly-looking mutt first,' Gaz demanded, glaring at Lara.

Ugly! Look who's talking, thought Lara, eyeing Gaz's four-chinned face.

'You let go of Spud and Star first, you big blancmange!' Ollie shouted.

'Calm down, everyone,' said Andrew, holding up his hands. 'Let's try to sort this out. What's going on, Guzzler?'

'This puppy has something of mine,' yelled Gaz, shaking Star in Andrew's face. 'And I want it back!'

'Her name's Star, you horrible man!' shouted Sophie, beginning to cry.

Andrew held up his hands again. 'OK. How about if Star hands over whatever she has, and you hand over the puppies. Deal?'

'Deal,' said Gaz.

Andrew held out his hand. 'Come on, Star, spit it out.'

Star opened her mouth and let a glittering, golden lump fall into Andrew's palm.

'There you are, Guzzler, there's your lump of gold. Now you –' Andrew stopped and stared down at his hand. 'Gold?' He looked up at Gaz again with a horrified expression. 'You're mining for gold here in Clearwater Valley?'

'Oh, that's really annoying,' grumbled Gaz. 'You could've all escaped to live another day. But now you know about Project Midas, I'm afraid I can't let you go. You'll have to come with me to Lakeside Mansion while I decide what to do with you.'

'Make us,' said Ben, sticking out his chin.

Gaz changed his grip on Spud and Star, sliding his big hands round their necks. The puppies began to cough and choke. 'One squeeze and their little necks will snap in half,' said Gaz with an evil grin.

'OK! We'll come quietly! Just don't hurt them,' begged Sophie.

'And tell your mutt to stay here,' ordered Gaz. 'She looks like she wants to take a bite out of me.'

Lara backed off and sat down, and in return Gaz loosened his grip just enough to allow Spud and Star to breathe.

'Don't worry, pups!' woofed Lara as the Cook children and Andrew trooped off to the mansion with Gaz bringing up the rear, still holding Spud and Star by their necks. 'Everything will be all right. I'll get you out of there!'

Lara resisted the impulse to take a great big bite out of Gaz's wobbly bum. Instead she turned and sprinted for the canoes.

15. Mud Monsters

The manager of the spa hotel walked down to the shore, checking that his gardener had cut the grass right down to the water's edge. He spotted a chocolate wrapper floating in the water and gave a disapproving tut. Folding back the sleeve of his expensive suit jacket, he fished the wrapper out. When he straightened up again, he was surprised to see a canoe heading straight for him.

'Stop!' he ordered, holding up his hand. 'You can't land here.'

The canoe kept on coming.

The manager started to repeat his order, but the words never came out. Instead, his mouth dropped open and he stared at the figure in the canoe. It was a black and white dog with a sticky-up ear – and it was paddling towards him as though its life depended on it!

'O-only human guests allowed,' said the manager faintly as Lara grounded the canoe and jumped out on to the grass.

'Don't worry,' she barked. 'I'm not planning on staying.'

The hotel manager jumped out of Lara's way, stumbled and fell into the lake.

'Stop!' he spluttered.

'Sorry,' woofed Lara, racing towards the hotel. 'I'm on a rescue mission!'

She shot across the patio and into the conservatory. A waitress screamed and dropped a tea tray, but Lara jumped clean over the mess, catching a cream cake in her mouth as she went.

'Mmm! Apricot,' she slurped.

The restaurant beyond the conservatory was crowded with guests. Lara tried to stop in the doorway, but the floor had been polished and she skated on, heading straight for a line of tables. She ducked her head and slid underneath, sending diners scattering.

When she emerged from under the last table, Lara turned. The guests were all sprawled on the floor, with dinner smeared across their faces, but Mr and Mrs Cook were not there. 'Please don't get up,' woofed Lara politely as she charged on towards the hotel spa.

Bursting through the double doors, Lara skidded up to the desk, where a bored receptionist handed her a towel without looking up. 'Thanks,' woofed Lara, slinging the towel round her neck and running her paw down the appointments sheet. Mr and Mrs Cook were booked in for a 'skin nurture' session, whatever that was. She turned round and saw a long corridor, lined with doors. 'Where do I start?' she groaned. 'At the beginning, I suppose.'

She galloped down the corridor and flung open the first door. The room beyond was full of steam. Lara wafted the clouds away to reveal a line of naked, sweaty people sitting on a bench. *I think they're nearly done*, she thought, scanning their bright red faces.

In the second room, a row of people sat in chairs, their faces plastered with white face packs and their eyes covered with cucumber slices.

'Hello? Mr and Mrs Cook? It's me, Lara,' she barked. 'Are you there?'

But none of the screaming, white-faced people seemed to recognize her, so she hurried on, checking room after room. By the time she got to the last door, Lara was beginning to panic. She had to find them soon! She charged into the room and nearly fell into a sunken bath full of sticky brown goo. Two mud-plastered people were sitting in the bath. They both stared at Lara, open-mouthed.

'Sorry,' muttered Lara, turning for the door again.

'Lara?' said one of the mud-monsters. 'Is that you?'

'Mr Cook? Oh, thank goodness!' barked Lara. 'We have to drive to Gaz Guzzler's mansion right now!'

'What's wrong, Lara?' asked the other mud-monster. It was Mrs Cook. 'What are you trying to tell us?'

Lara stamped her paw with frustration. Why couldn't humans understand Dog? She puffed out her cheeks and gave them an impression of an angry Gaz Guzzler. *Big man. Baddie.* The Spy Dog splayed her arms wide and walked forward menacingly. *Like a sumo wrestler?*

Mr Cook looked alarmed. 'There's a bear in the forest?'

Lara shook her head and tried again.

'There's a bear in the hotel?' guessed Mrs Cook, looking even more alarmed.

Lara slapped her paw to her forehead. If only she had something to write with. She looked at the white-tiled wall. *Of course!* Quickly, she scooped some brown gunge from the bath and used it to scrawl a message on the tiles.

Kids and pups held prisoner in Gaz Guzzler's mansion! Rescue now!

When Lara charged into the main lobby a few minutes later, the hotel manager was standing there, dripping pondweed on to the expensive carpet and shouting orders to his staff.

'I want this place searched from top to bottom!' he yelled. 'We're looking for a black and white dog with a sticky-up ear!'

'You mean that dog?' asked the bellboy as Lara galloped past, followed by two mud-monsters.

'Stop!' the manager spluttered, seeing the towel slung round Lara's neck. 'That towel is hotel property!'

But Lara and the Cooks were already sprinting across the car park, leaving behind them nothing but a swinging front door and a line of muddy footprints.

16. A 'Brief' Encounter

'Spy Dogs?' said Andrew, staring at Spud and Star. 'These two little pups are Spy Dogs?'

'Yes,' said Ben. 'Lara too. She's their mum.'

'They're part of a top-secret government project,' Sophie explained.

'But they live with us,' said Ollie proudly.

'Are you sure they're Spy Dogs? They don't *look* very dangerous.'

'What a cheek!' huffed Spud. 'I'm a highly trained lethal weapon, thank you very much!'

'Can you get your highly trained backside up here then, please?' yapped Star.

She was standing on the window sill of the bathroom where Gaz Guzzler had imprisoned them all five minutes earlier.

'What's the point?' said Spud. 'We can't get out. There are bars on the window – and we've already tried shouting for help. Nobody can hear us.'

'Yes, but somebody might *see* us,' said Star, nodding at the forest behind the house. 'Somebody like X and Hero, for instance.'

Spud's tail began to wag. 'Of course! They're still out there waiting for us to find them!'

Star nodded. 'We could signal for help using those dirty bed sheets in the laundry basket.'

Spud leapt up on to the side of the bath and yanked the sheets out of the basket on to the floor. 'Yuk!' he said. 'Those aren't bed sheets. They're Gaz Guzzler's ginormous dirty underpants!'

Star giggled. 'Never mind, we're only sending a brief message. *Brief* message. Get it?'

A few minutes later, with the help of the children and Andrew, they had a pair of Gaz Guzzler's enormous underpants tied to each half of the shower rail. Ben and Andrew stuck the pant-flags out of the window and moved them into the positions Star showed them, to spell out the word H.E.L.P. in semaphore.

When they had finished, Star scanned the forest. A bright light flashed from the trees.

'Yes!' she yapped. 'They saw it! They're signalling back with a mirror. It's morse code. "O – N – W – A – Y." They're on their way!'

'Let's hope they get here in time,' woofed Spud as the door opened and Gaz Guzzler stepped into the room, wearing a new set of clothes. He was pointing a gun at them. Before they could do anything, he reached out and grabbed Sophie by her hair.

'Oww!' cried Sophie.

'Let her go!' yapped Star, springing forward.

Gaz kicked Star across the bathroom floor. 'You and you,' he said, pointing to Ben and Ollie. 'Pick up those pesky pups and come with me.'

They trailed across the entrance hall of the

mansion, with Gaz Guzzler bringing up the rear, still holding Sophie by the hair.

'Open that door,' he ordered, waving his gun at Andrew. 'Then walk down the steps on the other side. And no funny business, or the girl brat gets it!'

They trooped down into the underground chamber where Spud and Star had surfaced after their swim through the underwater tunnel the night before. A steel cage stood open at the bottom of the steps. A few metres away, dark lake water lapped against the platform edge.

'In you go,' ordered Gaz. Silently, they stepped into the cage one by one. Gaz pushed Sophie in after them and then slammed and padlocked the cage door.

'What are you planning, Guzzler?' asked Andrew, looking up at the roof of the cage where the hook of a mini-crane was attached to the bars.

'Let me show you.' Gaz pressed the red button on the crane's control box. The crane arm lifted the steel cage with a jerk and swung it out over the dark water. 'Normally, we use this cage to lower mining equipment down to

the tunnel entrance,' said Gaz. 'But today, I'm going to lower you.'

'You can't do that!' Andrew shouted, shaking the bars.

'Oh, but I can,' hissed Gaz. 'It's all working out very nicely, actually. This way, I get to keep Project Midas a secret – and when you and these poor little children are found drowned on the shore after your tragic canoeing accident, the Tall Trees Outward Bound Centre will have to close! Oh, so sad,' he laughed, holding his belly in mock laughter. He stopped suddenly and his tone turned icy. 'I guess this is my final farewell!'

Sophie, Ben and Ollie crowded together for comfort, with Spud and Star held between them. Gaz pulled a lever and the crane began to lower the cage into the water, but just then a warning bell echoed around the chamber. 'Honestly,' grumbled Gaz, stopping the crane and looking up at the bank of CCTV monitors on the chamber wall. 'People always come to call at the worst times.'

'Look!' whispered Sophie, pointing up at the monitor that showed the gates of Lakeside Mansion. Three figures were hammering at the gates.

'That's Ma!' yelped Spud, spotting Lara.

Ben gazed at the two mud-covered people next to Lara. 'I'm not sure,' he said. 'But I think that might be Mum and Dad!'

Gaz Guzzler pressed another button.

'Yes, Boss?' Pete's voice echoed through the intercom system.

'Pete, I want you and the whole crew to stop mining and get up to the surface as fast as you can. I might need your help here.'

'Right away, Boss,' said Pete.

'Oh, and, Pete,' said Gaz, looking sideways at the steel cage. 'Don't come up through the tunnel. Swim to the shore in front of the house. I'll meet you there.'

Gaz switched off the intercom and threw the padlock key on to the bench. 'I'll be back as soon as I get rid of my other unwanted guests,' he said.

'Take your time,' yapped Spud.

Gaz waddled off up the concrete steps, grumbling all the way.

'That was close,' woofed Star once he had gone.

'So, how do we get out of here?' yapped Spud.

Just then, a nervous voice drifted down the

concrete steps. 'Garry? Coo-ee! Are you down there in your wine cellar?'

'That's how,' woofed Star, nodding in the direction of Mrs Guzzler's voice.

'Start shouting, everyone!' cried Sophie.

'We're locked up in a cage!' shouted Ollie.

'Please let us out, Mrs Guzzler!' yelled Ben.

'Oh dear,' called Mrs Guzzler. 'I'd like to help, but Garry doesn't allow me in his wine cellar.'

'This is no wine cellar,' Andrew shouted. 'Why don't you come and see for yourself?'

There was a long pause. Then they heard timid footsteps tapping down the concrete steps.

'Oh my goodness!' gasped Mrs Guzzler, as she stepped into the underground chamber. 'What is this place?'

'So you didn't know about Guzzler's – I mean Garry's – underwater gold mine?' Sophie asked.

Mrs Guzzler shook her head.

'Well, we knew,' said Ben. 'That's why he just tried to kill us.'

'Oh no, dear!' gasped Mrs Guzzler. 'I'm sure Garry didn't mean it.'

'You keep saying that, Mrs Guzzler,' said

Andrew. 'But Garry *did* mean it. Garry means everything he does – and everything he does is mean.'

Nice line, nodded Spud.

Mrs Guzzler's eyes filled with tears.

'He doesn't deserve a mum like you,' Ollie said sadly.

Mrs Guzzler let out a sob. 'Hang on, little boy,' she said. 'I'll have you out of there in a jiffy.'

17. Showdown

Gaz Guzzler stood at his front door, glaring down at Mr and Mrs Cook and Lara. If he could have folded his arms over his enormous belly, he would have done, but he couldn't reach. Instead, he settled for looking as stern as he could.

'This is private property!' he shouted. 'How did you get in?'

'We climbed over the gate!' Mrs Cook shouted back, marching up the steps towards him. 'What are you going to do about it?'

'Excuse me?' gasped Gaz, taking a step back. He couldn't see much of her face under the mud, but the bits he could see looked absolutely furious.

'Give me my children!' Mrs Cook yelled. 'You enormous oaf! *Now!*'

'And give me my pups while you're at it!' barked Lara, bounding up the steps.

'What children?' said Gaz Guzzler. 'I haven't seen any children.'

'You listen to me, matey,' growled Mr Cook, running up the steps to stand beside his wife. 'We're not messing around. If we don't get Ben, Sophie and Ollie back right now, we're going to ransack your house until we find them!'

'I won't let you,' said Gaz Guzzler.

'Oh yeah? You and whose army?' snarled Mrs Cook.

'*My* army, of course,' smirked Gaz, pointing to the lake where a dozen burly frogmen were wading to the shore. 'Pete! Escort these three trespassers out of the grounds!'

The lead frogman lifted his mask and nodded politely at the two mud-covered people with the black and white dog, as though it was something he saw every day. 'Would you like to come with me?'

'No, I most certainly would not!' snapped Mrs Cook. 'Your boss has kidnapped my children and I want them back!'

Pete looked shocked. 'Mr Guzzler?' he asked.

'She's lying!' said Gaz.

'No, she isn't!' yelled Ollie, running out of the house straight into Mrs Cook's muddy arms. Ben and Sophie followed him, each carrying half of a metal shower rail with a pair of enormous underpants tied to the end. Spud, Star and Andrew hurried out after them.

'How did you lot escape?' demanded Gaz.

'I let them go, Garry,' said Mrs Guzzler, stepping out of the house. 'They told me what you did to them. You've been a very naughty boy, son, but it's all over now.'

Sophie and Ben nodded, shaking their lengths of shower rail menacingly.

Gaz laughed. 'I don't think so. Get them, Pete.'

'I can't do that, Mr Guzzler,' said Pete.

'What are you? A man or a mouse?' yelled Gaz.

'I'm a miner,' said Pete with dignity. 'I don't hurt puppies, or kidnap children. I mine for gold.'

'Not any more, you don't,' snarled Gaz. 'You're fired!'

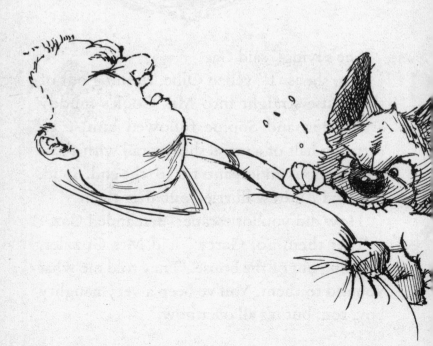

'No. I quit,' said Pete. 'Come on, men.'

The twelve frogmen marched off to a nearby minibus, climbed in and drove off, leaving Gaz standing on his own.

'I think you're outnumbered,' barked Lara.

Gaz Guzzler pulled a gun from his pocket. As he raised his arm, a furry black and brown streak flew out of the bushes behind him and fastened her teeth round his wrist.

'Owww!' shrieked Gaz, dropping the gun. 'Gerroff!'

Hero hung on, growling deep in her throat,

until X stepped out of the shadows, picked up Gaz's gun and signalled for her to let go.

'Does he ever take off that balaclava?' whispered Spud, nudging his sister.

Star giggled. 'I don't think so.'

'Time to use this,' said Gaz, hooking a gold chain out from under his shirt and holding up a little gold box for everyone to see.

'A bad-taste gold medallion?' woofed Lara. 'I don't see how that's going to help him.'

'This is a remote control,' said Gaz. 'It starts a timer that is attached to a bomb.'

'A bomb!' gasped Mrs Cook. 'Where?'

'Stuck to the side of Clearwater dam,' said Gaz. 'If I press this little ruby here, the timer starts ticking. Twenty minutes later – kaboom! The dam bursts and millions of tons of water pour down on to the towns and villages below.'

'You can't do that, Garry!' cried Mrs Guzzler.

'I can!' laughed Gaz. 'But – I won't . . . just as long as nobody follows me.'

Everyone stood back and allowed Gaz Guzzler to pass. Keeping their distance, they followed him down to the shore where his jet-ski was moored. When Gaz reached Andrew's canoe, he picked up a boulder and smashed it through the hull, shattering it into pieces. Then he clambered on to his jet-ski, started the engine and held up the little gold remote control. 'Oops!' he said, pressing the ruby button. 'I lied!'

18. A Chilling End

'Quick, Spud!' Star shouted. 'You defuse the bomb. I'll stop him!'

She grabbed the shower rail from Ben's hands and rammed it through a surfboard-shaped piece of the shattered canoe. Pushing off into the lake, she jumped on. Immediately, Gaz Guzzler's enormous underpants filled with wind. Star gripped the shower rail in her teeth and leant backwards as her makeshift windsurfer shot off in pursuit of the jet-ski.

'Way to go, sis!' woofed Spud, running for the spot where their scuba-diving gear was hidden. *No time for the wetsuit. And my oxygen tank is still lying empty on the tunnel floor.* He grabbed his mask and pulled it on. He reached for his tool belt, clipped it round his waist and flung himself into the lake. *More swimming!* The puppy powered through the water, heading for the dam.

Even swimming his fastest front crawl, it took Spud ten minutes to reach the great wall of stone at the end of the valley. His heart was pounding as he glanced at the stopwatch clipped to his tool belt. *Only nine minutes left!* He swam the curve of the dam, checking every centimetre of stonework as he looked for Gaz Guzzler's bomb.

Eight minutes to go. *Nothing!*

He swam it again. *Still nothing! The bomb must be under water!*

Six minutes left!

Spud spotted something red blinking in the murk below. He stuck his face in the water and peered through his mask. He saw a metal canister stuck to the dam wall. A timer on the side of the canister flashed numbers.

5.59
5.58
5.57

Spud yanked the screwdriver from his tool belt and slipped his paw into the special grip. His face mask was steamed up so he shrugged it off,

took a massive breath and plunged underwater.
The puppy kicked hard and reached the bomb.
He began to work on the first of four screws
holding the front panel in place.

5.01
4.59
4.58

The first screw came loose. Spud exploded to
the surface, gasped again and returned for
screw number two. *It's so difficult under water!*
And with paws instead of hands!

4.21
4.20
4.19

The third screw was rusted tight and he wasted precious time scraping the rust off before he could move it. He breathed one more lungful and returned for what he knew would be his final chance.

1.18
1.17
1.16

Spud's paws began to shake and the screwdriver slipped out of the fourth and final screw, scraping across the bomb surface. He was feeling light-headed. Finally, the fourth screw came free and the cover fell away into the depths of the lake.

1.00
0.59
0.58

There were six fat sticks of dynamite inside the cylinder, nestling in a tangle of wires. Spud took the pliers from his toolbelt and began to follow each wire, seeing where it went. Finally, he had isolated the two wires running between the timer and the detonator. One wire was red. The other was blue.

0.08
0.07
0.06

Spud moved his pliers to the red wire, and stopped. He switched them to the blue wire, and stopped. Which wire should he cut? The red or the blue?

0.04
0.03
0.02

Spud chose red.

Star's jaws were aching with the strain of holding on to the shower rail. The further she surfed out into the lake, the windier it got and the faster she went. She was closing the gap between her and Gaz Guzzler. His jet-ski engine was groaning under the strain of 160 kilos. If only she could hold on for long enough, she might be able to catch up and somehow make him stop the countdown sequence. *One thing at a time*, she thought. *First I have to reach him*.

Gaz Guzzler looked over his shoulder and spotted Star speeding towards him under a sail made out of his dirty underpants. His eyes widened with astonishment and fear. 'What are you?' he screamed. 'You're no ordinary dog!'

With a huge effort, Star managed to raise a paw and give Gaz an apparently casual wave. *Spot on*, she saluted. *A Spy Pup of the very rarest breed!*

'Get lost!' he yelled.

Star leant even further into the wind. The underpants snapped and billowed and she picked up speed.

With a roar of anger, Gaz Guzzler turned his jet-ski and headed straight for her. Star smiled to herself. *Perfect!*

Gaz sped past, sending a wave of water over her surfboard. Star hung on grimly. Gaz tried again, cutting even closer. Again, Star managed to stay afloat. The third time he came at her, she let her underpant-sail collapse into the water, braced herself on the board and opened the compartment in her collar. The blue Eazi-Freezi capsule fell out into her paw. *Come and get it*, she thought, watching the nose of the jet-ski loom towards her.

Star timed her throw so that the blue capsule landed right under the jet-ski. Instantly the water froze into a hard lump of ice and Gaz Guzzler came to a very sudden stop. He would have flown right out of the saddle, but his feet were frozen to his jet-ski.

'What have you done!' he howled. 'You stupid puppy!'

Star pointed at the little gold box round his neck. 'Press the button,' she woofed.

'You think I can stop the bomb with this?' Gaz whimpered, holding up the box. 'You're wrong! There's no Off button!'

Star felt her blood run cold as she thought of the thousands of innocent people in the valley below. It was all down to Spud now.

'Five seconds!' wailed Gaz Guzzler, looking at his watch and then at the dam, which was much too close for comfort. 'Four seconds! Three! Two! One! Mummeee!'

Star closed her eyes and waited for the bang.

'Funny time to go to sleep,' said Spud, skating beside her.

'Spud! You did it!' yapped Star, flinging herself on to the ice and hugging her brother.

'*We* did it, you mean!' said Spud. 'Spy Dogs forever, sis!'

19. Balaclava Bling

Professor Cortex smiled around at the little gathering of dogs and people on the beach in front of Tall Trees. X and Hero were cooking sausages at the barbecue. Hero wore an apron, and X was wearing his special party balaclava. It was lime green with diamante 'X's. Spud and Ollie were sharing a plateful of sausages and chocolate cake, Star and Sophie were playing frisbee, and Lara and Ben were sitting with Andrew and Mrs Guzzler, practising a few climbing knots. Mr and Mrs Cook were standing hand in hand, gazing out at the lake.

It was a beautiful early evening in Clearwater Valley. The setting sun shone across the water and the lake looked very peaceful. It had not been peaceful a few hours ago when the

professor and his agents had arrived by
helicopter. He had flown in from his top-secret
eagle-training base after receiving a coded
message from X. As the chopper had swooped
down over the lake, he had first spotted Lara,
the Cooks, Mrs Guzzler and Andrew on the

shore. They were all shouting and gesturing towards the dam. Next, he had spotted Gaz Guzzler bobbing up and down in the lake, frozen to his jet-ski like a human ice cube. A few metres away from Guzzler, Spud and Star were skating on the lake beside a pair of enormous underpants, laughing and hugging one another.

The chopper pilot had plucked Guzzler and his jet-ski from the lake with a grappling claw, and then flown to Clearwater Village with him suspended underneath. 'Put this criminal on ice!' Professor Cortex had called as the chopper dumped Gaz in front of the police station. 'Oh, wait a minute. He already is!'

Now Professor Cortex chuckled, remembering his own joke. 'That was one of my better efforts,' he said to himself as he tapped the side of his glass with a spoon.

Everyone gathered round. Professor Cortex cleared his throat and beamed at them. 'On behalf of the British Government, I would like to thank you all for your brave efforts today. Because of you, the Clearwater dam is safe, and thousands of people are peacefully going about their business in the valley below. X and Hero,

148

you were as cool and professional as ever. I would expect nothing less.'

Everyone clapped as X and Hero each gave a dignified bow.

'And he can cook!' yapped Spud, waving his sausage. 'Lovely grub – and not a grub in sight!'

'Nice bling too,' woofed Star, pointing to X's sparkly balaclava.

'Ben, Sophie and Ollie,' continued Professor Cortex, 'Andrew tells me you were all very brave and resourceful this afternoon. Well done!'

Again, everyone clapped. 'Mum and Dad were brave too!' called Sophie.

'Especially you, dear,' said Mr Cook, making Mrs Cook blush. 'You were a tigress!'

'Yes, thank you, Mrs Cook,' said Professor Cortex. 'And I'm sorry that you and your family were put into danger again.'

'That's all right, Maximus,' said Mrs Cook. 'It wasn't your fault – this time! And I must admit I quite enjoyed getting stuck in. Nobody hurts my children and gets away with it!'

'Hear, hear!' woofed Lara. 'Mums united!'

'What about Andrew and Mrs Guzzler?' called Ben. 'Andrew stood by us all the way.'

'And Mrs Guzzler did the right thing, even

though it was very hard for her,' added Ollie, slipping his chocolate-smeared hand into hers.

Mrs Guzzler gave a wobbly smile. 'I've promised Garry I'll visit him in prison. I'm afraid he'll be in there for a very long time, but I'm hoping he'll lose a lot of weight and gain a lot of manners! In the meantime, Andrew and I have an announcement to make.'

Andrew cleared his throat. 'Mrs Guzzler has agreed to work here at Tall Trees with me.'

'Yes, it's about time I looked after some more deserving children,' said Mrs Guzzler, once everyone had finished cheering. 'And I'm using some of Garry's millions to close down the mine and clean up the underwater village. The lake in front of Garry's mansion will be open to anyone who wants to use it!'

'And last, but definitely not least,' said Professor Cortex proudly, 'our three amazing Spy Dogs: Lara, Spud and Star. Once again, you saved the day and caught the baddie. Cheers!'

'Cheers!' everyone shouted, raising their glasses.

'Spy Dogs forever!' barked Lara, Spud and Star.

Their cheers rose up into the air, drifted out

across the lake, where an otter lay on his back gazing up at the stars, and floated away over the dam and into the valley below, where thousands of lights twinkled in the windows of thousands of houses.

It all started with a Scarecrow.

Puffin is seventy years old.
Sounds ancient, doesn't it? But Puffin has never been
so lively. We're always on the lookout for the next big
idea, which is how it began all those years ago.

Penguin Books was a big idea from the mind of
a man called Allen Lane, who in 1935 invented
the quality paperback and changed the world.
**And from great Penguins, great Puffins grew,
changing the face of children's books forever.**

The first four Puffin Picture Books were hatched in 1940 and the
first Puffin story book featured a man with broomstick arms called
Worzel Gummidge. In 1967 Kaye Webb, Puffin Editor, started the
Puffin Club, promising to **'make children into readers'**.
She kept that promise and over 200,000 children became
devoted Puffineers through their quarterly instalments of
Puffin Post, which is now back for a new generation.

Many years from now, we hope you'll look back and
remember Puffin with a smile. **No matter what your age
or what you're into, there's a Puffin for everyone.**
The possibilities are endless, but one thing is for sure:
whether it's a picture book or a paperback, a sticker book
or a hardback, **if it's got that little Puffin
on it – it's bound to be good.**